DOUBLE-BARRELED SHOWDOWN

The cowboys watched curiously as the eight riders came up, all abreast. Without a word spoken by either side, they dismounted. Then before the cowboys could blink back their astonishment, the eight whipped back their long linen coats and yanked short double-barreled shotguns from their belts. The guns had bores that looked to be as big as tomato cans.

Bulldog had his squinty eyes fixed on Will. He said, "I told you we ain't allowin' no goddam Texas cattle around here."

"Well, we're here," Will said.

"Not for long you ain't. You round up them bony brutes and git them across the river or we'll do it for you."

Shaking his head, Will said, "Not just yet."

Bulldog took a step closer. "Then by God, you'll die right now."

Will tried to sound brave, but his voice was wavery. "Why don't you and me fight it out? You got guts enough for that?"

Bulldog's lips skinned back in a cruel grin. "I could whup you with one hand, but we ain't got time. Say your prayers, cowboy. . . ."

DODGE CITY TRAIL
DOYLE TRENT

ZEBRA BOOKS
KENSINGTON PUBLISHING CORP.

ZEBRA BOOKS

are published by

Kensington Publishing Corp.
475 Park Avenue South
New York, NY 10016

First printing: September, 1990

Printed in the United States of America

Chapter One

He didn't belong here. These wild-bearded, smelly, loudmouthed buffalo hunters weren't his kind of men. He wished he hadn't stopped at Adobe Walls. It was the promise of some woman-cooked meals and grain for his horses that had persuaded him to stay overnight.

Now he was fighting for his life.

They were out there. Hundreds of them. Comanches, Cheyennes, Kiowas, Arapahos. And they were crazy with hatred of white men. Inside the three sod buildings were twenty-eight men and a woman. The men were well armed with their long-barreled buffalo guns, and they were dead shots. But they were outnumbered about twenty to one, and none of them expected to see sundown.

Will Porter sat on the wooden floor of Hanrahan's Saloon, surprised that the first attack had been beaten back. The Indians had carried away some of their dead, but were forced to leave at least three bodies behind. They were gathering to charge again. Any second now.

"They got the Shadler brothers," a bearded buffalo hunter said. "They was asleep in their wagon and never had a fightin' chance."

"Shore 'nuff," said another. "I seen them bucks drag their carcasses out of the wagon and cut off their hair."

5

"They'll be comin' back. Come on boys, let's see what else we can find to shove up against this door."

They had already pushed some tables against the wooden door, and now a dozen men grunted, swore, and dragged the long wooden saloon counter up to the door.

"Good thing these walls are made out of dirt or they'd burn us out."

"Wonder how they're doin' over there in the stores?"

"Dunno, and I ain't about to run over there and find out. There's some bucks layin' out there in the grass just waitin' for a white man to stick his head outside."

Will Porter had put his new Winchester repeating rifle down to help move the saloon counter, and now a dirt-streaked buffalo hunter picked it up, turned it over, and allowed, "This ain't nothin' but a toy." He turned his gaze to Will. "What does she shoot, kid, little ol' .44s?"

"Yeah," Will answered. ".44-40s."

"Hell, a man carries a real gun. Like this 'un." He held up his Sharps .50 caliber. "This 'un'll knock a buffler over at six hunnert yards. It'll knock an Injun over a mile away."

"Yeah," Will said, taking the Winchester out of the man's hands. He didn't want to argue, so he said no more.

A bugle sounded from somewhere near the bank of the South Canadian River. It was a tuneless, senseless noise.

"Like to get that sonofabitch in my sights," a hunter muttered.

"He had to of took that horn off of some dead soldier."

"They're a-comin' agin, boys. My gawd, look at 'em."

They came. Most on horseback, but some on foot. All but a few had rifles and pistols. The shooting began. Buffalo guns boomed and rifles cracked. The shooting

6

was so fierce it sounded like one long, continuous explosion. Only the crazy, blood-freezing screams of the savages cut through the racket.

They swarmed around the three buildings, shooting, screaming, beating on doors with rifle butts. The barricaded doors held. Some of the Indians backed their horses into the doors, trying to bust them in with horsepower. Still, the doors held.

Will Porter squatted under a narrow window until a buffalo hunter fired his long-barreled rifle and stepped aside to reload. Will raised up, got a savage in the sights of his Winchester, and squeezed the trigger. The savage fell face down. In a second, Will had another cartridge levered into the firing chamber, and he aimed and fired again. A lead slug whined past his right ear and knocked a puff of dirt off the far wall.

He was shoved aside when the hunter had his rifle reloaded, and he waited until the hunter fired and ducked back. Without hesitating, Will again took his place and shot a painted Indian who was poised to poke a rifle barrel through the window. When that Indian fell another popped up no more than two feet away. Quickly levering in another shell, Will fired point blank.

A man yelled above the noise, "There's that goddamn Quanah Parker. Over there on the gray horse. Git that sonofabitch."

Will looked through the window and saw him. He'd heard about Quanah Parker, fighting chief of the Comanches. His mother was a white woman who had been kidnapped by the Comanches, and had become one of them. Her son was the most cunning and bloodthirsty savage in the southwest. As Will watched, the gray horse fell with a .50-caliber bullet in its heart, and the Indian chief was pitched off. But before anyone could draw a bead on him he scrambled behind the horse's body and stayed down.

"Come on," the hunter beside Will muttered. "Show

7

your head, you goddam sonofabitch.

The big Fifty Fifty boomed, deafening Will, and the hunter swore, "Goddamit. The sonofabitch ducked." He stepped aside to reload.

Looking through the window, Will saw the Indian chief jump up and run. He had the Winchester to his shoulder, got the Indian's back in his sights.

But he didn't shoot.

Then he noticed that the gunfire from outside was slackening. Another voice yelled, "They're a-leavin', boys. They're pullin' back."

"Yeah, by God," someone said, "we whupped 'em agin."

The buffalo guns continued booming until the enemy was out of sight behind a low hill. Finally, the shooting stopped. Will Porter sat on the floor under the window, weary, wishing it were over, knowing that it wasn't.

He should have shot that Indian chief. Why didn't he? He sat with his knees up and his arms folded across his knees. He put his head on his arms.

What was he doing here, anyway? He was no buffalo hunter nor Indian fighter. He was a cattleman on his way to Dodge City. He wished to God he'd never stopped here. He had no quarrel with the Indians. Everyone knew the government peace commissioners at Medicine Lodge had promised the Indians that buffalo hunters would stay out of the Texas Panhandle. Now here they were, killing buffalo by the hundreds. The buffalo were everything to the Indians; food, shelter, clothes, even weapons. Before they got hold of white men's rifles, the Indians made their bows and arrows out of buffalo bone and sinew. Hell, if he were Quanah Parker he'd be fighting mad, too.

The night before, while he was trying to sleep on the saloon floor, he'd heard the hunters brag about how many "buffler" they'd killed. One black-bearded, stinking hulk said he could kill two hundred "buffler" a day and keep fifteen skinners busy. No wonder they'd killed all the buffalo in Kansas and were moving south.

Will Porter raised his head and looked at the men around him. No one was down. No one seemed to be hurt. An ugly bunch of men. Except for one or two. The youngest one, a kid they called Bat, was fairly decent looking. What was his last name? Masterson. Yeah, Bat Masterson. And the other one was Billy Dixon. Will had heard of him. He was an army scout as well as a buffalo hunter, and one of the best marksmen in the country.

With all the bullets that had slammed into the outside walls and poured through the windows, it was unbelievable that no one had been hit. Lucky that they were all awake at the first light of dawn when the Indians attacked. It was a cracking ridgepole supporting the roof that had awakened them. At least that's what Hanrahan said.

"The ridepole's busted, boys," he'd yelled. "Damn ridgepole's busted."

Every man in the saloon jumped up. Some climbed on tables and chairs and reinforced the ridgepole with their hands. Others went outside, climbed up on the roof, and shoveled dirt off to lighten the load on the ridgepole. Then after more lanterns were lit, a close examination showed the thick pole was still strong.

"It's that goddam Jim Hanrahan," someone muttered. "He's scared of the Injuns and he wants ever'body awake."

By that time a pale early-morning light had spread over the flat grassy land, and suddenly someone shouted, "Good gawd a-mighty. Look over there."

The warriors were lined up in attack position, two deep, awaiting the signal. "Good gawd a-mighty. There's a thousand of 'em."

"At least five hunnert," a man said.

"We're in for it, boys."

Two shots were fired out the windows to warn the

men and a woman in the other two buildings. And the attack began.

The first one lasted about forty-five minutes, and Will Porter did his share of the shooting. He took careful aim and tried to make every shot count. The Winchester held fifteen bullets and that was all he had with him in the saloon except for the five in his pistol and four more in loops on the pistol holster. After the second attack he was worried. He'd have to run for the corrals by the blacksmith shop to get more ammunition out of his pack panniers. That would be dangerous. Damned dangerous. He'd have to. He couldn't just sit on the floor and do nothing while the battle raged on. He was thinking maybe he ought to do that now. Now would be as good a time as any. He stood, about to announce his plan, when Billy Dixon spoke:

"It's that medicine man they call Isatai. He's the one talked 'em into killin' us all. See that paint on 'em? He's got 'em believin' he knows how to make bullet proof paint."

"Isatai? What does that mean in white man's talk?"

"It means coyote shit," Dixon answered. "He's one mean sonofabitch. But when he run up against Old Quanah, he more'n met his match. He ain't about to take over from him."

"Goddamit," a hunter said. "I was plannin' on makin' my pile this summer shootin' buffler, but them goddam Injuns are makin' life miserable for ever-'body."

"Maybe the army'll run 'em off. Old Miles has got the soldier boys and the cannons and he can make sausage out of 'em."

"Yeah, if the gen'ral gov'ment in Warshinton'll let 'im."

"Well shit that ain't gonna do us no good if we cain't git out of here."

Will Porter figured he had two cartridges left in the

Winchester. He spoke to the room. "I'm gonna have to run over to the corrals and get some bullets out of my packs."

"Shit, they'll fill you so full of lead it'll take a mule to carry you back."

"You gents keep a lookout and if you see an Indian raise up out there, shoot him. I'll make it."

It was the youngster, Bat Masterson, who said, "We'll do 'er, mister. Run like hell." As young as he was, Masterson seemed to have the respect of everyone there. Will believed he could be depended on.

Taking a careful look outside the window, Will climbed out. He lifted himself onto the windowsill with his hands, reached back for his rifle, and put one leg outside and then the other. For a moment he crouched under the window. It was about a hundred yards to the blacksmith shop and the corrals. He unbuckled the spurs from his boots to make running easier. He shifted the rifle to his left hand and lifted his Russian .44 six-gun out of its Slim Jim holster, cocked the hammer back. He stood and ran.

Chapter Two

A rifle bullet hit the ground near Will Porter's feet, and a buffalo gun roared behind him. Head down, willing his feet to move faster, he didn't look back, didn't look anywhere, just ran. Another bullet zinged past his head and another tore a chunk off a wooden picket as he reached the corral. Behind him the hunters were returning the fire.

Instead of crawling between the pickets, Will hit the ground on his belly and rolled under them. The corral gate was open and his horses were gone. All the horses were gone. But his saddle and packsaddle and panniers were still lying in a corner where he'd left them. Bending low, he opened the left pannier, fumbled through the canvas, and found a box of .44-40s. He shoved the box in his pants pocket, rolled under the corral, and ran again.

Bullets zinged past him. Buffalo guns boomed. A white man shouted, "Over here."

Glancing up, Will saw that one of the store buildings was closer than the saloon, and he turned in that direction. Men were looking through an open window, guns ready. Running as hard as he could go, Will reached the side of the building and tried to dive headfirst through the window. He got his head and shoulders inside, and strong hands pulled him the rest of the way through. He fell in a heap on the floor, still hanging onto his two guns.

Someone said, "Mister, that was the craziest damfool thing I ever seen. What're you tryin' to do, anyways?"

"I, uh . . ." He had to get his breath before he could answer. "I was almost out of bullets. Had to get some more out of my packs."

"Wal, mebbe it's best you did. We need all the guns and bullets we can git."

Will looked around the room. There were five men and the woman. Mrs. Olds, he'd heard her called. She and her husband ran the restaurant. She was a good cook. "Anybody killed here?" Will asked.

"Nope. Not yet. But it ain't over. Not by a damn sight."

Mrs. Olds spoke: "The Lord has watched over us. He's watching over us now." She was known as a religious woman and she was calm.

The building was one of the stores. Crates of tinned food and sacks of flour and sugar were piled against the door. The men were bearded, except for one. Will guessed he was Mrs. Olds's husband. "They ran the horses off," Will said. "We're afoot."

"Yeah, we seen 'em. Couldn't do a damned thing about it. Excuse me, Mrs. Olds, I didn't mean to cuss."

She sat in a wooden chair, weary. "The Lord will take care of us." She wore a dress that came down to her button-up shoes. Her brown hair was bunched into a knot at the back of her head.

"Shore," a man muttered through his beard, "the Lord and this buffler gun."

She stood again. "I'll find something to eat."

"Keep low, Mrs. Olds. They're still out there."

The woman rummaged through some boxes of groceries at the back of the building, used a can opener to cut open four tins of sardines, then opened a box of soda crackers. "Come and eat."

"Not everybody at once," her husband said. "Keep a lookout."

Will and a hunter in baggy bib overalls kept watch while the others ate. When they were spelled, they went to the rear of the store and ate with their fingers. "What's your name, mister, and what're you doin' here?" The hunter spoke around a mouthful of sardines and crackers.

A crooked grin turned up one corner of Will's mouth. "My name is Will Porter. I was headed for Dodge City and I stopped here to get the wrinkles out of my belly."

"You a cattleman?"

The hunter was looking him over, squinting at him. What he saw was a young man, obviously a cattleman in his brown duck pants and blue cotton shirt, with a big black silk bandana tied loosely around his neck. Will Porter was a little above average in height, and slender, with the lean hips of a cowboy. When he pushed his hat back a shock of sandy hair fell across his forehead. Normally smooth shaven, he had a two-day growth of sandy whiskers now. The hump in his nose, broken when he bumped heads with a horse, ruined what otherwise would have been a handsome face.

"Yep. I left fourteen men and two thousand and eight hundred head of beeves back there on the Pease River."

"Headed for Dodge, you say? I ain't never heard of nobody shippin' cattle at Dodge."

"We heard the railroad got to Dodge City a couple of years ago."

"Yup, the Atchison, Topeka and Santa Fe, but I ain't seen no cattle around there."

"Maybe we'll be the first."

Conversation died. Will and the hunter ate as fast as they could, fearing another attack would cut their meal short. The other hunters didn't know how to talk without swearing, and they didn't want to swear in

14

front of the woman. While he ate, Will wondered whether the Indians had discovered the men and cattle he'd left behind. All he could do was hope. The cowboys were armed with Winchester repeating rifles and six-shooters and they'd put up a good fight. But against a hundred or more warriors they wouldn't have a chance.

It was a dry year. Terribly dry. The grass wasn't growing, and everywhere a trail herd had passed the grass was cropped off. Now it was almost July and still no sign of rain. They'd been on the trail, up from West Texas, about forty-five days, and the cattle were shrinking.

Will's uncle, Lucas Porter, was worried. "We're losing a pound per head every day," he said, shoving his hat back and scratching his thin, gray hair. We're gonna have to throw off the trail somewheres and let 'em graze. If we don't we ain't gonna have nothing left but hide and bones when we get to Wichita."

"How about Dodge City?" Will asked. "We know the railroad's there. We know that much. And that's a hell of a lot closer."

They had talked about Dodge City before, and the possibility of selling cattle there. But they knew no cattleman who had ever been there and they didn't know what to expect. They'd decided to go on to Wichita or Ellsworth, where many trail herds had gone ahead of them.

Lucas Porter didn't answer immediately, but Will could tell by the way he pulled his chin down and stared at his horse's ears that he was thinking about it.

"And we wouldn't have to go through the Indian Nation," Will added, "and we wouldn't have to worry about that quarantine. They ain't quaranteed that far west yet. Dodge City would be better."

"Weel, that's what we heard, but we ain't sure."

"A lot of cattle have been driven up to Kansas, quarantine or no, but you can't tell, the John Laws up there might decide to enforce it."

"Weel, we just don't know what's at Dodge City. We could drive a hell of a lot of cattle up there for nothin'.'"

Two days later they swam the Pease River, and Lucas Porter ordered the cowboys to throw the herd off the trail. "There's a wide valley over west about four miles and the grass there ain't been cropped off. We're gonna have to hold 'em up there 'till they put on some weight and strength."

That night after supper, the older Porter called his nephew aside, and they walked away from the chuck wagon and cooking fire. When they were out of earshot of the crew, Lucas Porter dug his tobacco out of a vest pocket and rolled a cigarette. Will knew he had something to say, and waited for him to say it.

Finally, "What we was thinkin' about Dodge City might be right but we don't know." He lit the cigarette with a wooden match, pinched out the match, squeezed it in his hand, snapped it in two, and dropped it. "Here's what I want you to do. . . ."

So Will left early next morning, riding a good bay horse and leading a brown packhorse carrying a few groceries and his canvas-wrapped bed. He rode a day and a half and knew he was in the Panhandle when he swam the South Canadian. He'd heard of Adobe Walls, but he'd heard only that it had been abandoned by the buffalo traders and was nothing but ruins. He hadn't heard that it had been rebuilt. It was a good place to stop overnight, get some good chuck into his own belly, and something besides dry grass for his horses.

It seemed like a sensible thing to do.

"Hyar they come, fellers."

Will dropped his cracker and ran over to one of the two windows. He had to squeeze in beside a hunter to look through. Just as before, they came by the hundreds, shooting, screaming. And as before, guns roared and the noise was painful to the ears. Mrs. Olds sat on the floor and held her hands over her ears. Her lips moved silently.

A hunter stepped back from a window to reload, and Will took his place. His Winchester dropped a painted buck. He levered in another round. Before he realized what was happening a young warrior stuck his arm through the window and emptied a six-shooter into the room. His shooting filled the room with gunsmoke, but every shot missed. When the warrior's gun clicked on empty, he turned and ran. Will's bullet hit him squarely between the shoulders.

But the Indian didn't fall immediately. Instead he staggered about a hundred feet, then fell.

"That little pea-gun ain't got no killin' power," a man muttered. "Let me at 'im."

Will watched as the young brave rolled onto his stomach, pulled another pistol from his belt, and fired several shots at the building. Then, just before the hunter was ready to squeeze the trigger, the warrior turned the gun around and shot himself in the head.

"Well, I'll be gone to hell," the hunter said. "I never seen nothin' like that."

Gunfire continued. Buffalo guns boomed from the three buildings. Rifles cracked and pistols popped. A bullet hit the window frame near Will's head and dry dirt was kicked into his face. He dragged a shirt sleeve across his eyes and got the rifle to his shoulder again. The Big Fifty beside him went *kapow*.

"I got 'im," the hunter yelled. "I got the sonofabitch with the horn. See 'im-a-layin' out there."

Sure enough, a man wearing white man's pants and a buckskin vest was down, flat. A bugle lay beside him. The man had hair like a . . .

"Good gawd," the hunter yelled. "A nigger. He's

17

a nigger."

"I heard about him. He done run away from the army."

"Wal, he ain't a-runnin' no more."

Rifle butts beat on the door. A horse was backed into the door. The door latch split and the door opened a few inches. When a warrior's face appeared in the opening, a pistol shot knocked him back.

Then a savage arm came through the opening, and at the end of it was a brown hand holding a six-shooter. A slash with a skinning knife made the savage jerk his arm out without firing a shot.

The attack went on. When he had a chance, Will glanced around the room. No one was down. Unbelievable. A bullet knocked off his new Stetson, and he left it where it fell. Gunsmoke was so thick in the room it stung his eyes. He and two hunters were taking turns firing out the window.

Finally, when the sun was low in the west, the shooting outside stopped.

"We whupped 'em, we whupped 'em. We, by God, shot the hound dog—excuse me, Mrs. Olds—we shot the devil out of 'em."

"The Lord is watching over us."

"Think they'll come back, Lem?"

"Not tonight. Injuns don't like to attack in the dark. They'll sneak around in the dark like a coyote and cut your throat if they get a chanct, but they don't attack."

"We must of kilt a hunnert of 'em."

"Mebbe. But there's four or five hunnert more. They ain't givin' up yet."

Will Porter sat on the floor and shoved bullets into the side of the Winchester. It was going to be a long night. No one would get much sleep.

And tomorrow the fighting would begin again.

Chapter Three

When dark came, the men had some discussion about whether to light the lamps. If it was light inside, an Indian who sneaked up to the window would have easy targets. If it was dark, a savage could sneak up to the window without being seen.

They decided to leave the room dark, but keep a man wide awake at each window. At the slightest suspicion, the guards were to yell a warning. Will Porter lay on the dusty wooden floor and tried to sleep. His was the third watch. His hat, his new Stetson, was his pillow. It had a bullet hole in it, and lying on it flattened it, but it was made of good beaver fur and could be straightened again.

Grinning to himself in the dark, he hoped he'd get a chance to show his uncle and the cowboys the bullet hole. He was proud of that hat, with its round crown and flat brim. Flat until he'd had to use his black silk muffler to tie it on in a strong Texas wind. That was why so many cowboy hat brims were rolled up on the sides.

That bullet hole would be something to talk about. If he stayed alive.

It was black inside the store. He couldn't see his hand in front of his face. A hunter struck a match to light his pipe, and was soundly cussed. "Goddamit, man, you

19

wanta git kilt. Excuse me, Mrs. Olds."

The match was immediately extinguished.

Will was glad he hadn't picked up the smoking habit. He'd heard too many men light a pipe or a cigarette and say, "Well, reckon I'll drive another nail in my coffin."

A man whispered, "Whose turn is it? I cain't hardly keep my eyes open."

A shuffling of feet, and, "I'll take 'er. Heard anything?"

"Nary a thing."

Will must have slept a little because the next thing he knew someone was whispering, "Who's next. Hey, in here, who's next?"

"Huh?" Will snorted awake. "It's me. It's my turn." He groped his way to the window.

"Keep your ears open. Be daylight in a couple hours. That's when they like to hit."

"Sure, you bet."

"Keep that little popgun ready."

Staying awake was easy. Will was too scared to be sleepy. He blinked in the dark and strained his ears, trying to catch every sound outside. The wind picked up and moaned around the corners of the building. Damn. That made it harder to hear anything else.

What was that? Every sense Will Porter possessed was alert. There it was again. A scraping noise. Something shuffling along outside. An Indian.

Pistol cocked, holding his breath, Will waited, eyes and ears straining. Should he yell a warning? No, not yet. He didn't want to make a fool of himself.

It moved again. Something or someone was out there. He could hear it move, stop, then move again, scraping the ground. He listened. The wind moaned.

Now it was under the window outside. Will's heart was in his throat. Should he shoot, shout, or what? He was about to yell a warning when he heard it move. It went past the window and on down the street.

"Huh." Will let his breath out with a whoosh. A

tumbleweed. Or something. Blowing in the wind. Sure. He grinned a crooked grin. Scared half to death by a damned tumbleweed.

Or was it? The grin left his face. Probably. Hell, probably wasn't good enough. But damn, no way to be sure. Well, if an Indian poked his head in the window he'd be sure. If he could see him. Suppose it wasn't a tumbleweed?

Gripping the pistol in his right hand, Will carefully put his left hand out the window. Fearfully, he moved the hand around. If there was an Indian there he could only hope he'd feel of him before the Indian could grab his hand.

His hand came into contact with the windowsill and nothing else. Again, he let his breath out, and realized his heart was beating too fast. Well, he was young, only twenty-five, too young to die of heart failure.

Come on daylight.

He was weak in the knees and ready to collapse when the eastern horizon showed a faint, pink light. A whisper came from behind him, "Don't shoot, kid, it's me." A hunter loomed up beside him. "Hear anything?"

"Naw."

"Soon be light enough to see."

"Yeah."

"Go ahead and lay down. I'll stay here. Shit, cain't sleep nohow."

"All right."

He sat on the floor and leaned back against a wall. He was tired, as tired as he'd ever been in his life. With his rifle across his lap, he let his head fall back against the wall and let his eyes close. When he opened them again, it was daylight.

A man said, "See any Injuns, Lem?"

"No live 'uns. There's some dead 'uns out there."

"Reckon they'll come again?"

"Mebbe. Mebbe not."

"Wonder if anybody was hit over at Leonard's and the saloon."

"Dunno. If I don't see any live Injuns purty soon I'm goin' over there to find out."

They waited. All was quiet. Then a man appeared in the street between the buildings, a white man. It was Billy Dixon. Another white man showed up behind him. The door at Leonard's store opened and the two were joined by still another bearded hunter, carrying a long-barreled Sharps.

When Dixon walked near the window, a hunter yelled, "Whatta you think, Billy?"

"I think," drawled Dixon, "that them bucks found out they wasn't bulletproof after all."

"Think they'll come again?"

"Who knows."

And then a yell, "There's some. Over yonder. A bunch of 'em."

Will looked where the man was pointing and saw them, a half dozen braves sitting on their horses away over south, their heads turned in the direction of Adobe Walls.

"They're gittin' ready to come again."

"Say," Dixon said to one of the hunters, "let me borrow your gun."

"What for?"

"I think I can shoot one of them sons of bitches right off his horse."

"Hell, you can. That's gotta be a mile away."

"Let me try."

"All right. She's a .50-90 Sharps, Billy. She's got a double trigger."

Dixon took the rifle and knelt on one knee. He put his left elbow on his left knee and held the rifle barrel in his left hand. He squinted down the barrel, then lifted his head and raised the high rear sight. Squinting again, he held his right cheek against the gun stock, pulled the first trigger. That cocked the gun and got it ready to fire. His finger on the second trigger now, Dixon squinted, took a breath, held it, squeezed the trigger.

Kaboom.

"Jaysus H. Jones, Billy," a man yelled, excited. "Did you see that? Did you see that?"

"Knocked 'im right off his horse," another man yelled. "Good God a-mighty, I cain't believe what I seen."

"Man, that's one for the books."

"Look at 'em go. Picked up the dead 'un and hightailed it."

"Well," Dixon drawled, handing the gun back to its owner, "they know for sure now that they ain't bulletproof."

"Think they'll come back?"

"Can't say, but I kinder doubt it. They know now that old Coyote Shit's magic ain't workin'."

Men poured out of the three buildings and gathered in the street. A grimy, bearded, ragtag bunch of men, carrying their long-barreled rifles.

"They got Bill Tyler," a man said somberly. "Took a bullet in the throat. Took 'im a hour to die."

"Anybody else?"

"None that I know of."

"That's three, then. the Shadler brothers and Bill Tyler."

"Reckon how many we kilt?"

"They packed off most of their dead, but there's some dead 'uns out there."

"They run off the hosses."

"Yeah. We're afoot. We cain't go nowhere afoot."

"We gotta have help. Hope somebody comes along with some horses."

Billy Dixon shook his head sadly. "We're stuck here, fellers, till somebody shows up with horses and we can send somebody to Dodge for help."

"Yup, that's the way of it, boys. If them redskins caught us tryin' to walk to Dodge, out in the open, we wouldn't last ten minutes."

"Anyhow," the bearded James Hanrahan put in, "I ain't gonna leave my propity here for them damned savages to tear up."

They ate a cold breakfast, still afraid to wander very far from the buildings. But by noon, when a live Indian hadn't been seen since dawn, they became bolder. They muttered, swore, and stomped around in their jack-boots and overalls, watched the horizon in all directions, and swore some more. In the late afternoon, they began counting the dead Indians. There were thirteen.

Then a buffalo hunter unsheated his skinning knife and cut off a dead Indian's head. Grinning, he carried the head by its long hair to the edge of a shallow draw near the saloon and stuck it in on the end of a stick. With the help of another hunter he pushed the stick into the ground, leaving the head staring grotesquely toward the South Canadian. Other hunters did the same, and soon all thirteen heads were lined up above the ground on sticks.

It made Will Porter sick.

He could only choke down his supper, and he carried his bedroll from the saloon to Rath's store for the night. When it came to an Indian fight, the buffalo hunters couldn't be beat, but the rest of the time they were too bloodthirsty, loudmouthed, dirty, and smelly to suit Will Porter. He vowed he'd get away from them as soon as possible.

Outside, over near the blacksmith shop, was a pile of buffalo hides waiting for a wagon to haul them to Dodge City and the railroad. Sooner or later someone would come along with a wagon, either a hunter or a trader from Dodge City. Will would be among the first to leave.

At daylight, he ate a breakfast of Mrs. Olds's good cooking, trying to keep his mind off the dead Indian heads, then walked outside by himself. He had to get

24

away from the hunters, at least for a little while. He turned his steps north, away from the bloody heads.

Carrying his two guns, he walked, his eyes on the horizon and on a brushy draw to the north. As he approached the draw he hesitated. It could hide a dozen savages. Well hell, a man had to relieve himself out of sight of Mrs. Olds. The outdoor toilets stunk so bad he couldn't stand them. The brush was better.

With slow, careful steps, he pushed into the brush. Oak, he believed, with green leaves so dense he couldn't see what was on the other side. He had to know before he put his rifle down and unbuttoned his pants. He took six more steps, and saw the Indian.

Chapter Four

Will Porter froze, afraid to move farther. His eyes were fixed on the Indian until finally he realized it wasn't moving. It was on its back. Dead. Still, the young man was afraid to move. He stood there, every muscle, every nerve bunched. Where there was one Indian there were more.

No.

When it occurred to him, he relaxed. The savages had carried away most of their dead. This one had been overlooked. That meant there were no more Indians around. Feeling safe now, he pushed on to the far side of the brush, stepping around the dead warrior, and stopped to unbutton his pants.

He saw the horse.

"Wha?" he said, surprised. "Hey, Rascal. Rascal, you old sonofagun." It was one of his horses, the brown packhorse. The animal had an Indian war bridle on its head, nothing more than a thin leather headstall, a leather thong in its mouth, and one long rein. The rein trailed on the ground.

"Rascal. Boy am I glad to see you. What're you doing here all by yourself, anyway?"

The horse's head was up and it watched him approach, but didn't try to move away.

"Did some Indian try to make a war pony out of

26

you?" And when he thought about it he knew what had happened. The warriors had opened the corral gate and stampeded the white men's horses, but one warrior who needed a mount caught Rascal. Later, the warrior was shot, but managed to stay on the horse until he got into the brush. There, he fell off and died. Rascal had stepped on the rein and stayed put.

Grinning, Will scratched the animal's neck. He looked it over carefully and saw no wounds. "I'll be damned," he said happily. "You're worth a thousand dollars right now. Hell, a million."

Every man and the woman turned out to look when Will led the horse back to the buildings. "What'll you take fer 'im, mister?"

"He's not for sale," Will said.

"What're you gonna do with 'im?"

"I'm riding for Dodge."

"Well," Billy Dixon allowed, "somebody has to go for help. Will you do that, kid? Will you send back some men and horses?"

"Sure, you bet. I'll get there as fast as I can."

"It's about a hunnert and fifty miles. The trail's easy to see."

"Shit, that means we're stuck here for at least six days. Excuse me, Mrs. Olds."

Will was saddling the horse. He would have to travel light, leave his bedroll and most of his groceries behind. When he had his Texas double-rigged rimfire saddle cinched in place he unrolled his bed, picked out two blankets, and spread them on the ground.

The slab of bacon he had in one of his panniers was still good. After taking a careful smell of it to be sure, he rewrapped it in heavy brown paper and placed it in the center of the blankets. The bread had some gray spots, and he pinched that off and placed it beside the bacon. A skillet, he had to have a skillet. He picked the smaller one from his pannier, and a box of wooden matches.

"We got some airtights you can take," Mrs. Olds said. "If you ain't got no money to pay for 'em I'll loan you some."

"I can pay," Will said.

She hurried to one of the stores and came back with four cans of fruit and three cans of sardines. Will rolled it all up in the blankets and tied the blankets behind the cantle of his saddle. He shook his canteen to make sure it was full and hung it on the saddle horn.

"Listen, kid," Billy Dixon said, "I'm guessin' old Quanah headed south to the north fork of the Red River, but I'm only guessin'. The country between here and Dodge could be full of Injuns. Keep your eyes peeled and sleep with a gun in your hand."

"Fort Dodge is just east of Dodge City," a hunter added. "Tell 'em we need fightin' men and horses."

Will shoved his Winchester into a boot under the right stirrup fender, then buckled on his once-discarded spurs. He picked up his reins and swung into the saddle.

"Adios, gentlemen." He started to turn the horse and ride away, but then he thought he ought to say something else. He grinned a crooked grin. "If I ever get in a gun battle again, I hope you gents are on my side."

Mrs. Olds said, "The Lord'll be with you, young man."

He touched spurs to the brown horse's sides and rode away at a trot. He pushed through the scrub oak in the draw and kept going, ignoring the dead Indian and looking in all directions at the same time. He saw nothing threatening. A half hour later he reined up, turned in his saddle, and looked back. The sod buildings were far behind him, barely visible on the Texas prairie.

With a wry grin, he said to himself, "If I live to be a hundred and fifty, I'll never forget that place."

*   *   *

A fire could be seen for a long way, and Will Porter didn't want to be seen. He ate a cold supper that night of canned sardines, stale bread, and a can of peaches. His horse was hobbled and sidelined nearby and was cropping the buffalo grass. The grass was brown but plentiful, and the animal would get enough to eat.

Rolled up in his blankets, Will listened to the night breeze rustle the grass and to the sound of the horse grazing. It was a dark night. The sky was full of stars but there was no moon. Unless he had been spotted by an Indian before dark, he was safe for the night. He slept.

By sunup he was on his way again. The wagon road was easy to see, and that worried him. If Indians were looking for white men's scalps they would be watching the road. He reined off and kept going northeast, staying parallel with the road and about a mile east of it. He wondered if the road was part of the old Santa Fe Trail. Probably was. At noon he stopped, unsaddled the horse so it could rest better, and ate a can of tomatoes.

When he came to the Canadian River, he turned west again to the wagon tracks, where the crossing was easy. It wasn't quite swimming deep, and he took off only his boots, fearing to strip and make himself look foolish if he was spotted by Indians. Then he went on, traveling at a steady trot, letting the hot prairie winds dry his clothes. A hundred and fifty miles, someone had said. That meant another night of sleeping on the prairie. He ought to get to Dodge City by the end of the next day.

The country was rougher now, prettier, with rolling hills and shallow ravines. Yucca, with its jagged green spikes, was everywhere, but there was plenty of grass, too. Grama, buffalo, and the tall bunchgrass. And yellow prairie flowers. But the land was dry. It needed rain. He guessed he was now crossing a narrow strip of the Indian Nation, and soon he would be in Kansas. He followed a buffalo trail down into a ravine and up the other side. There he stopped to let his horse blow.

And saw the man.

Immediately, Will Porter dropped off his horse and drew the Winchester out of the saddle boot. The man was about a quarter mile east in the ravine. By straining his eyes, Will could see he was wearing a white man's clothes, baggy clothes and a big floppy hat. He was a little man, no bigger than a boy. And there was a horse. No, two horses. Not another living creature was in sight.

The man was down in the same draw that Will had ridden across, and was bent over, working hard at something. Curious, Will mounted and turned his horse in that direction. The man was working so hard digging with a shovel that he didn't see Will approach. Four shallow holes had been dug in the sandy bottom of the ravine. Looking for gold? Naw. Will had never heard of anyone finding gold in Kansas.

"Hey," he yelled when he got closer. "Hello."

The man's head jerked up and the shovel fell from his hands. Moving fast, he picked up a long-barreled rifle.

"Hey, I'm a white man. Don't shoot. I'm harmless." Will sat his horse, looking down into the ravine.

"Who . . . who are you?" The voice was high, thin, scared.

"My name is Will Porter. I'm headed for Dodge City. Who are you?"

"Are you alone?" He was young, a boy, too young to shave.

"Yeah, I'm alone. I'm harmless."

For a long moment, they studied each other. The boy was scared. Fear had turned his face white, and his hands on the rifle trembled.

Seeing that, Will forced a grin. "I'll put my gun down if you'll put yours down."

"Well . . ." He hesitated, then said, "All right, but you put yours down first." Will shoved the Winchester back into the saddle boot.

"And your pistol. Put it on the ground." Will

30

dismounted, lifted the Russian .44 out of its holster, and carefully placed it on the ground.

"He said, "If I come down there will you shoot me?"

"No. Not if you're careful." The boy was still talking in that high, thin voice.

Leading his horse, Will made his way into the ravine. He couldn't stop staring at the boy. He asked, "What're you doin', kid? Are you all by yourself?"

"Yes. Yeah." He still gripped the rifle, but it was pointed at the ground.

"Well . . ." Glancing around, Will saw the remains of a campfire about fifty feet away and a rolled-up canvas-wrapped bed. A skillet sat on the ground by the dead ashes. "Excuse my curiosity, but what are you doin'?"

The boy snapped, "That's none of your business."

"Huh?" Will was surprised at the quick answer. He pushed his hat back, reset it, and studied the boy some more. Couldn't be more than fifteen. Sixteen at the most. In baggy corduroy pants, laced shoes, a plaid shirt at least three sizes too big, and a broad-brimmed black hat pulled so low it covered his hair and pushed the top of his ears down. The hands were small with slender fingers. Dirty.

"Well, I reckon if you don't wantta tell me that's your business. But don't you know there's Indians in this country that'd trade their best pony for your scalp."

"I haven't seen any Indians."

"Well, I sure as hell have. I hope I left 'em behind me, but I can't be sure."

"Where?"

"Adobe Walls. There were four or five hundred of 'em, all with nothin' on their minds but killin' white folks."

"Adobe Walls? I've heard of that place."

"You're gonna hear a lot more about it. If you live long enough."

They were silent a moment, still looking each other

31

over. He reminded Will of when he was fifteen. He'd tried his best to talk and act like a man, but couldn't fool anyone. That seemed to be what this kid was doing, talking strange, acting strange.

"I can't begin to guess what you're up to, kid, but if I was you I'd get on those horses and hightail it for Dodge City. Sooner or later some of those bloodthirsty Comanches, or Cheyennes or whatever they are are gonna spot you and eat you for supper."

The boy thought it over, looked at the ground, back up at Will. "Maybe . . . maybe you're right."

"I'll help you load your packhorse. We can travel together. That'll give us two guns if we have to fight Indians."

"All right."

Will caught one horse while the boy caught the other. "Which one do you ride?"

"This one."

The boy had a cross-buck saddle and panniers with straps and buckles. Will saddled the horse, a small bay, while the boy loaded his camp supplies in one of the panniers. "Naw, that's not the way to do it," Will said. "You have to balance the load and try to keep those bags flat on the inside, the side next to the horse. It's easier to tie 'em down that way."

Nobody spoke as Will rearranged the load in the panniers. Then Will offered a small apology. "On second thought, these bags are so light it won't make much difference. You wasn't planning on staying out here long, was you?"

No answer.

"I started out with a packhorse, but the Indians got away with him. I was damned lucky that the brave that stole this horse got shot off of him."

"Were there any white people killed?"

"Three. That's hard to believe, I know, but that's all."

They mounted and rode out of the ravine. The boy

had his bedroll and shovel on top of the packhorse. A last cinch and the straps and buckles crossed on top of the load held it in place.

Riding silently, Will glanced back at the boy now and then, but said nothing. At a trot, he could see that the boy was bouncing up and down in his saddle and was uncomfortable. He could do nothing about that.

They followed another buffalo trail across another ravine, rode to the top of a low hill, started down it. "Uh-oh." Will reined up suddenly.

"What? What is it?" The boy stopped besided him.

"Did you see 'em? Indians. At least three. down there. They ducked behind that hill when they saw us, but they'll be comin' after us." Will turned his horse around. "We'd best get back to that arroyo where we've got some cover.

The boy stared at him as if he couldn't believe it.

"Dammit, kid, come on. Let's lope."

Chapter Five

Will Porter took off at a full gallop. When he looked back, he saw the boy was having trouble getting the packhorse to run. Will took down his catch rope, reined his horse around behind the packhorse, and whipped it over the rump. All three of the horses got into a full gallop then and kept it up until they were sliding to the bottom of the sandy ravine. Dismounting, Will pulled the Winchester from its boot and climbed back to the top. He flattened out on the ground and watched back the way they had come.

"They saw us, all right," he said. "They know right where we are. We're in for a fight, kid."

The boy was on the ground, gripping his long-barreled rifle. His face was white with fear again. "How . . . how many are there?"

"Four. That's all I can see now. Might be some more somewhere. Get up here and get that gun ready. They're comin'."

The boy scrambled up beside Will and lay on his belly. "What, uh, what . . ." His lower lip was trembling so badly that that was all he could say.

"Dammit," Will said, looking over at the boy's guns, "that's one of those sport rifles, ain't it? Do you know how to shoot it?"

"Yes. I, uh, I've fired a few rounds for practice."

"Well, it's better than nothing'. Fact is, maybe it'll shoot farther than this one. Let them get a little closer and try to hit one."

34

"Do you mean shoot them."

"Why, hell yes, I mean shoot 'em. What do you think we're doin', playin' hide-and-seek?"

"I've never, uh . . ."

"You never shot anybody?"

"No."

"Well, that's no disgrace, but goddam, kid, you have to shoot. Kill them or they'll kill us. Here, let me see that gun." He took the rifle out of his hands. "Got any shells?"

"Here." He handed Will a box of long, thin cartridges. Without looking to see what caliber they were, Will broke open the breech of the rifle, shoved a cartridge into the firing chamber, and cocked the hammer back. He put the gun to his shoulder, then lowered it again. "What kind of goddam sight is this?"

"It's called a peep sight. You get the front sight in that little hole."

"Oh. Yeah." Will squinted down the barrel again and muttered, "Just come a little closer, you sons of bitches."

"Are you going to just shoot them down?"

"I sure as hell ain't gonna wait for them to come and shoot us."

They came on, four of them, riding thin horses, moving cautiously. They had long-barreled rifles decorated with eagle feathers. One of them was wearing a white man's muslin shirt, but was bare legged. Another had on a white man's dark pants, and was bare chested. Will got the bare-chested one in the gun sights.

But he didn't shoot.

Could they be friendly? Naw. There were no friendly Indians. But maybe they didn't want to fight. Maybe they . . . what? They'll kill us if they can, he thought. Only four of them.

Will raised the rifle barrel and fired a shot over their heads. The Indians stopped suddenly, sat their horses a moment, talking among themselves. Then they dismounted and spread out, keeping about fifteen feet apart. Bending low, rifles ready, they walked with determined steps toward the white man and boy.

Two of them fired. The bullets fell short.

"Goddam," Will muttered. "The lead's gonna be flying around here, kid. Here, take your gun and get ready to shoot back."

With trembling hands, the boy took the gun and managed to reload it. Will put the Winchester to his shoulder and waited. The Indians kept coming, slowly, carefully. Will squeezed off a round. The Winchester cracked and the recoil had a good solid feel. But the distance was too great for accurate shooting. One of the Indians heard it go past and hit the ground on his belly. From a prone position, he fired, and Will heard that bullet go past. "See if you can pick one off with that sport gun," he said.

He didn't look to see if the boy obeyed, but he heard the rifle cartridge explode. At least the kid was shooting.

The Indians were all on their bellies now, crawling in the grass, trying to get closer without making targets of themselves. Will took careful aim and fired. He saw a puff of dirt near an Indian's left foot. The Indian raised up on one knee and fired back.

"Damn," Will muttered, "those warriors know how to fight." The long-barreled rifle went off next to him.

Gunfire came rapidly from the Indians now, and one of the warriors, wearing buckskin leggings, ran, bending low, to Will's left. Will knew he wanted to get down in the ravine and come up behind them. If he did, they would have to keep a watch in two directions. They'd be caught in a squeeze. Couldn't let him do it. The Winchester cracked again.

The warrior hit the ground face down, and Will thought he'd missed. But then the red man's arms and legs flailed, pounded the ground, and then he flopped over onto his back and lay still.

While he was watching, a bullet kicked dirt in Will's

36

face, blinding him for moment. The rifle beside him popped again. Will had to put down his gun and use his black silk muffler to wipe dirt from his eyes. When he got his eyes open, the Indians were retreating, crawling backward.

"Pour it to 'em, kid. Give 'em billy hell." He fired the Winchester at the same time the sport rifle next to him popped. The three live Indians stood and ran, bending low. Will and the boy watched as they ran to their horses, jumped on the horses' backs, and rode away at a gallop, leading the dead warrior's horse.

"Whoo," Will grunted, wiping his eyes with the muffler again.

"Why are they running? There are still more of them than there are of us."

"They don't wantta pay the price. They didn't know what they had cornered here, but they soon found out we ain't takin' no shit from nobody."

He saw the boy wince, and he wondered if he shouldn't have used dirty language. Maybe the boy was one of those Holy Rollers who never swore. Well, hell, how was he supposed to know. "Tell you what, kid, I'm goin' over and have a look at the one I shot. Keep your eyes peeled in case they come back."

"Yes, of course."

On top of the ravine, Will advanced toward the prone body, his rifle ready. But the body didn't move, and when Will got closer he saw the hole in its left side. Blood had poured out of the hole, but the bleeding had stopped. A handsome warrior, wearing handsome buckskin leggings and a beaded band around his throat. The black hair was parted in the middle and pulled to the back of the head and tied there. The face was dark and hairless. The dark eyes were open, sightless.

Shaking his head sadly, Will said, "I wish all this hadn't happened. I wish you didn't hate white folks so much. Sleep easy." Picking up the fallen rifle, he saw it was a Henry, a Civil War Yankee gun. It had a lever-action loading mechanism, just like his new Winchester, and when it worked right it could fire as fast as his Winchester. But the Henry had a reputation for jamming. The stock was covered with buckskin, laced on, painted with a red circle and two red parallel lines. Two feathers from a red-tailed hawk were tied to the barrel with a leather string.

Will glanced back at the boy. The boy was standing, looking in the direction the Indians had gone. He jacked the lever down on the Henry and saw that it worked. He pumped the lever until two cartridges were flipped out. That was all it held. The Indian had had two shots left. Maybe that was why his pals ran. They couldn't just walk into a store and buy ammunition, and they had none to waste.

Well hell, he thought, they should have left us alone, then they wouldn't have wasted any ammunition and nobody would have got killed.

"What shall we do?" the boy asked when he walked back.

"Reckon we'd better get on our way. They know where we are and we don't want 'em coming back with some help. Let's get as close to Dodge City as we can. Who knows, we might see some other white men."

"Yes. There is safety in numbers."

He glanced at the boy, then led the way back down into the ravine. He tied the Henry on top of the packhorse's load beside the shovel, mounted, and picked up the packhorse's lead rope. The boy mounted his bay horse. When they were out of the ravine and traveling northeast, Will glanced at the boy again.

"You did some shootin'. Ever shoot at a human before?"

"No. And I missed."

"Well, I missed a couple of shots too, but you let 'em know we had some firepower."

"Some people think the Indians aren't human."

"Yeah."

"What do you think, Mr. Porter."

"It's Will, not mister, and I don't know what to think. They look like humans, and they act like humans. I never knew an Indian personally, but I reckon they are human." Afraid of another question, Will got the horses into a steady trot. The boy followed, bouncing in the saddle.

They stayed east of the wagon road, and every time they topped a rise Will looked for it, not wanting to lose it. The country was flat again, with only low hills. A few cottonwood trees grew in small bunches where water stood part of the year. Tall yellow sunflowers grew on the hillsides, and the short prairie and grama grass was thick in places. Thick but brown. The whole Southwest needed rain. Will expected to see buffalo, but there were none, and he mentioned this to the boy.

"I've heard," the boy said in his strange voice, "that the buffalo are getting scarce in Kansas, and the hunters are moving south."

"I reckon that's why they built up Adobe Walls again."

They jogged on, the boy hanging onto the saddle horn with both hands now. Before dark, Will picked out a spot near some cottonwoods and reined up. "There's wood for a fire, but I'm afraid to build a fire. Too damned many redskins around. There's grass for the horses, but no water. Ain't seen any water since mornin'. We'll let 'em have a taste out of our canteens. Hope we can keep 'em strong in case we get in a horse race with a bunch of cutthroat Comanches. Or Cheyenne. Or whatever breed runs in these parts." The boy slid from the saddle and almost collapsed. "You're not used to ridin', are you kid?"

"No." That was all the boy said while Will offsaddled and hobbled the horses. He remained quiet while they ate the rest of Will's tinned food and some bread and dried beef the boy had in his panniers.

"Go easy on the water, kid. Save some for the horses." He held his finger over the hole in his Stetson and filled it with water from his canteen. Then he allowed each horse three swallows and no more. "A horse'll drink fifteen gallons of water a day some days," he allowed. "A thirsty horse can empty a five-gallon can in a couple of minutes. All we've got left is what's in your canteen."

The boy said nothing.

"You don't talk much do you?" No answer, only a shake of the head. "I told you my name. What's yours?"

"Uh, uh, Lou."

"Lou?"

"Yes."

"Well, if you don't wantta tell me your full name that's your business. Right now I've got some business of my own to take care of." He walked away, stopped beside the thick trunk of a tree, and started to unbutton his pants. Looking back, he saw the boy stand quickly and walk hurriedly in the opposite direction. That is one strange damned kid, he mused silently.

Dark came on, and Will rolled up in his blankets, fully dressed except for his boots. The boy had a better bed, with a tarp, blankets, and even a pillow. He carried it a short distance away before unlacing his shoes and crawling into it. Lying on his back in the dark, his hands under his head, Will picked out the Big Dipper, the Milky Way, and the Little Dipper. The night wind rustled the leaves in the cottonwood trees. It was a peaceful sound. He looked over at the boy, but could barely see him in the dark. Strange kid. Strangest kid Will had ever seen. Wouldn't talk any more than he had to. Digging holes in the prairie and wouldn't say why. Wouldn't take a pee where anyone could see him.

Suddenly, Will sat up. "Hey," he said to the dark prone form about thirty feet away. "Hey, I know what's wrong with you."

"Uh, what did you say?"

"I said I know what's wrong with you."

"Uh, what?"

"You're a girl, that's what."

40

Chapter Six

Lucina Mays had been a family problem as a child and still was a constant source of worry. Never interested in dolls and playing house, she should have been a boy. Always more interested in boy sports, always wrestling with her two older brothers and sometimes winning. She had gone to good schools in Kansas City and knew how to be a lady, but somehow tea parties and fancy dresses bored her.

When she was born, her mother was pleased to have a daughter, and named her Lucina after the Roman goddess of childbirth. Ironic. At twenty-two, she still hadn't thought much about having babies. Her father was a merchant, a storekeeper, and so was her grandfather on her mother's side. Grandfather Mays had also been a merchant, but a man with adventure in his soul, an entrepreneur who didn't mind taking a risk, financially and physically. Though dead for ten years, he still was Lucina's idol, her hero. She wanted to be like him.

But dammit, no one would take her seriously. When she finally voiced her feelings and ambitions at the family dinner table one night, she was answered at first with nothing but shocked silence, then finally a few scoffs and snorts from her father and brothers. And her mother's crying.

"All right," Lucina had shouted, "why can't I? Why can't I have my own business and be my own woman? What law says a woman can't manage a business as well as a man?" She stomped out of the dining room, angry and frustrated. But when she heard her mother crying she went back and put her arms around her mother from behind. "I'm sorry, Mother. I don't want to be a heartache for you. I'm just not . . . I'm afraid I'm a little abnormal. Please don't worry. I love you, Mother."

Talking about being her own woman was one thing, doing it was something else. It took money to be an entrepreneur. A body had to have something to start with. Borrow? Hah. Most successful businessmen were men who had an idea and put their own money with what they could borrow and went to work on it. As Grandfather Mays had once said, "You figure out what people are willing to pay for and you provide it. If you have to borrow to do it, fine. Then two of you will make money. You and the banker."

Sure. If you're a man. A woman? Hah. She had a little money of her own, but not enough, and she couldn't borrow a dime if her life depended on it.

Well, she'd do it anyway.

When she boarded the train for Dodge City, she had a plan. She hoped it would work. It had to work. She'd by golly make it work.

With help from Grandfather Mays.

Now she was disappointed. So far she had accomplished nothing, and to make matters worse, the Indians were on the warpath. When she'd bought the horses and equipment she was advised that the Indians were anything but friendly. Still, she didn't believe she was in very much danger until the young man came along and told her about the attack at Adobe Walls. And sure enough, the two of them were attacked by Indians. It was fortunate that there were only four Indians, and that she and the young man had been well

42

fortified in that ravine. It was also very fortunate that she wasn't alone at the time.

But what was she going to do now?

It was the young man stomping around in his boots and spurs that awakened her. He was coming back from looking at the horses, and he squatted before one of her pack panniers. Well, she could stop acting now. He knew.

"Good morning," she said, no longer trying to disguise her voice.

Without looking at her, he said, "Mornin'."

"I have some coffee in my packs. Can we make some coffee?" She pushed the blankets and tarp down and put on her shoes.

"Naw. Smoke can be seen a long ways on this prairie. We'll have to eat what we can without a fire and get going. We ought to get to Dodge City by dark."

"Boy," she said, standing in her baggy, shapeless clothes, "won't that be wonderful."

He looked up at her then. "How long you been camped out here?"

"Three days. And three nights."

"What're you doing, anyhow?"

"I can't tell you."

"Well, go ahead and keep your mouth shut. I don't care." He bit off a hunk of bread and spoke around a mouthful. "Why the hell—heck—should I care?"

She ate silently. He acted as if she weren't even there. She saddled her horse, but allowed him to saddle and load the packhorse. Neither spoke again until they were a half mile from where they'd spend the night, and he said only, "I hope we come across some water soon. These horses need it." At noon they stopped and tried to get the horses to graze, but they were too thirsty to be interested in dry grass. They went on.

It wasn't until midafternoon that he spoke again. "There's s'posed to be a creek around here called Mulberry Creek. That's what I was told. Sure like to

43

see it."

"I've heard of it, but I don't know where it is."

Silence. Only the hoofbeats of the horses. Then she glanced at him and said, "You're a cattleman, that's obvious, but why are you going to Dodge City?"

A mischievous grin turned up one corner of his mouth when he looked her way. "That's none of your business."

"Oh. I understand. You are absolutely right. Forgive me."

They came to some water late that afternoon, and it wasn't a mere creek. "That's got to be the Arkansas," Will said. "Dodge City is on the Arkansas."

"Yes. It is. That much, I know. We can't be far away, but which way do we go?"

"West. The wagon road is west. First we've got to water these horses."

The railroad was there, complete with a one-story depot, well built of good wooden siding, and a water tank on high wooden legs. A huge pile of coal for firing the steam engines sat on the east end of town. They would have to burn coal, Will Porter thought. There aren't many trees around here. The lumber used to build a bridge across the Arkansas and the row of houses had to have been hauled here from somewhere east by the railroad.

Also piled near the railroad were buffalo hides, waiting shipment to the tanneries in the east. One pile was as big as a three-room house, and it stank. The old Santa Fe Trail was the main street, and the street was lined on one side with buildings, mostly one-story with false fronts, and a few two-story. A plank walk ran in front of the buildings. On the other side of the street was the Atchison, Topeka and Santa Fe Railroad.

"There are some livery pens on the west side," Lucina said. "I'm staying at the Dodge House." They rode past the hotel's wide front porch. Across the top of the

44

porch was a sign that identified the two-story building as the Dodge House, and adjacent to that, under the same roof, was a sign that read: Billiard Hall.

A wagon loaded with buffalo hides went past them in the opposite direction. Two more freight wagons were going west ahead of them. The sidewalk was well used by bearded men in baggy overalls and floppy hats. There were a few ladies in long dresses, and an assortment of men in derby hats, fedora hats, wool vests, and wool pants, with staches and muttonchop whiskers. No cattlemen. Some of the pedestrians watched Will and the girl ride past, but showed only mild curiosity.

"I don't see no stock pens," Will said in a half mutter.

"What? Stock pens? No, I don't recall seeing any."

Will's jaws were clamped, and he said no more until they dismounted at a livery barn.

"Say, Miss Mays," said a short man in baggy clothes when they rode up, "I was gettin' worried. Thought the Cheyennes got you."

"I'm fine, Mr. Easton. Tired, but fine."

"Whatever prodded you into goin' off by yourself like that, anyhow?"

She didn't answer. Will spoke: "Is there an army around here? I left a bunch of men afoot down at Adobe Walls. We fought off a hell—heck—of a lot of Indians down there, and the Indians ran off all their horses."

The short man's jaw dropped open. "The hell you beller. Injuns, you say? Anybody killed?"

"Three white men and I don't know how many Indians. Somebody said they were led by Quanah Parker. Is there a fort around here?"

"Yeah. Over east a ways. Good gawd. And there's white men still down there?"

"Yeah. They're afoot. They need help."

"Gawdamighty. I'll go spread the word at the

saloons. We'll git a army together and git down there."

"I'll go with you as soon as I take care of these horses."

Miss Mays was forgotten as Will and the livery owner hurried down the main street. Pedestrians on the plank walk saw the harried expressions on their faces and got out of their way. Dodge City had grown rapidly since it was platted two years earlier, and now had two restaurants, a liquor store, a hardware store, a blacksmith shop, four mercantiles, a hotel, a barber-shop, and seven saloons.

They stopped first as the Longbranch Saloon, a long, narrow room with a bar on one side and tables at the rear. Coal oil lamps were suspended from the ceiling. A dozen or more men who looked like buffalo hunters stood at the bar while some well-dressed gents played cards at the tables.

"Hey, ever'body," Easton yelled, "Adobe Walls was hit by old Quanah. Three white men was killed and about twenty-five men and a woman are still down there afoot."

"What? What's that you say?" They gathered around. "Tell 'em young man," the livery owner said. "Tell 'em what happened."

Will told them. He didn't like talking so much, but the story had to be told. They fired questions at him, and he answered patiently. "A woman, too?"—"Yeah. Mrs. Olds, they called her."—"Why I know her. Runs a damned fine restaurant. Who else?"—"Well there's a man named Billy Dixon and a young feller called Bat Masterson, and a saloon keeper named Hanrahan, and I don't know who all else."—"Billy Dixon? He's a fightin' fool."—"So's Bat. He's a good 'un."—"We got to git down there. Git your guns, boys."—"It's a three-day ride. Best wait 'till mornin'."

From saloon to saloon, Will and Easton went, and everywhere the excitement was high. Men were more

46

than willing to ride out immediately, but were talked into waiting for morning.

In the last saloon, Will again answered questions: "How many Injuns?"—"It was hard to tell, but I'd guess at least three hundred. Some of the men said there was more than five hundred. All I can say is I never saw so many Indians, or any other men, at one time."—"Are you givin' us a song and dance?" The questioner was a buffalo hunter and smelled like it. "No. It's hard to believe, but it's true. I came up here on business, but if you need me I'll go back with you."— "You better be tellin' the truth, mister." Will Porter shook his head sadly. "It's the truth."

By that time weariness had set in and Will wanted a good supper and a soft bed where he wouldn't have to worry about Indians sneaking up in the night and cutting his throat. The Dodge House, she'd said. He knew where that was. Carrying his roll of blankets, he went there, stepped up onto the wide porch, and went inside. It was one of the most elegant places he'd ever seen, with a big parlor and a dozen padded chairs. The woman behind a long desk looked him over carefully, but with a friendly face. The rate was a dollar fifty per day or eight dollars per week for room and board, she said.

"I don't know how long I'll be staying," Will said. "Would it be all right if I pay by the day?"

His room on the second floor overlooked an alley and a row of wooden shacks on the other side of the alley. It was dark by then so he lit a lamp on a small table. On another table was a porcelain washbasin, a bar of soap, and a towel. A small mirror hung on a wall over the table. He had nothing to unpack, so he splashed water over his face and went looking for the restaurant. Tonight he'd take a bath in the water closet on the first floor and tomorrow he'd get a barbershop shave. Then he'd . . . what? Well, he'd have to ask

47

questions until he found someone who had some answers. What he'd seen so far didn't look encouraging.

In the restaurant he was seated at one of a dozen tables. All kinds of men sat at the other tables, from dirty hunters to well-dressed businessmen. The waitress was pretty, with chestnut hair coiled at the back of her head. She wore a long white apron over her gray dress.

"Would the gentleman prefer buffalo steak or beef?" she asked, and when he gave her a quizzical look she added, "I can guess by your boots and spurs that you'd prefer beef."

Grinning, he said, "Right now I could eat anything, but make it beef, will you?"

He was halfway through his meal of beefsteak, mashed potatoes, gravy, and corn when he happened to glance up at the doorway and see a girl standing there. A pretty girl, with dark hair parted on the side and combed down to about chin level, where it ended in an upward curl. Her dress was white with a lacy front clear down to her slippers. There was lace at the collar and cuffs, too. Every man in the room was staring. A very pretty girl. At first he didn't recognize her, and when he did he gulped down a mouthful of food and stared himself. He couldn't believe it.

It was her.

Chapter Seven

When she saw him she smiled, and it was the kind of smile that someone had paid plenty of dentist bills for. Her dress was pinched in at the middle and curved out in the right places.

And he once thought she was a boy?

Finally, he realized he was staring and turned his head.

But when she approached he had to put his fork down and stand—and stammer. "Good, uh, evenin', uh . . ." Come to think of it, the livery owner had called her Miss Mays.

"Good evening, Mr. Porter. May I join you?"

"Sure. Of course. Sit, uh, please have a seat."

It occurred to him he should pull out a chair for her, but she didn't give him time. Instead she pulled out a chair herself and sat opposite him. "Please go on with your meal, Mr. Porter. I don't mean to interrupt."

"Will. My uncle is Mr. Porter."

"Will, then. Call me Lu. My full name is Lucina Mays, and I'm from Kansas city."

"All right, Lu."

She sat up straight, primly, with her hands clasped together on the table, and studied him. He felt his face grow red, and he didn't know what to do with his hands.

Finally, she said, "Down there on the prairie you knew how to talk to me." A small smile turned up the corners of her mouth. "You haven't had much experience with young ladies, have you Will?"

"Huh? Why, sure. Sure, I've known some girls, uh, young ladies."

"Texas is a big state. You are from Texas, aren't you? Where in Texas did you come from?"

"West Texas. On the Pecos River."

"How did your break your nose?"

The question was so direct that it caught him by surprise, and again he stammered, "Why . . . I got hit by a horse's head, I mean, well, I was puttin' a bridle on a horse and a feller said somethin' to me and when I looked at him the horse slung its head to throw the bit out of its mouth and its jaw cracked me on the nose." Whew. That was a long sentence.

She smiled, showing those white, even teeth again. "I've always wanted to meet a cowboy."

"You've never met a cowboy?"

"No. I've seen Texas cowboys at the stockyards in Kansas City, but I never got to meet one."

Grinning sheepishly, he said, "You haven't missed a whole lot."

Her smile widened. "What are you doing in Dodge City?"

His sheepish grin turned into a crooked one. "What was you doin' down there in that arroyo?"

Her smile slipped and her hazel eyes turned serious. "Honestly, I can't tell you. I don't mean to be mysterious, but I just can't. I apologize."

He studied her face, realized she meant what she'd said, and shrugged. "Well, there's nothing mysterious about me. I've got—my Uncle Lucas has got two thousand and eight hundred head of cattle cropping the grass down on the Pease River. We was headed for Ellsworth or Wichita, but decided to drive 'em here instead. That is, if we can ship 'em from here."

50

"Oh really?" Her eyebrows went up. "Now, that's interesting. Hmm. And you believe, now that the Atchison, Topeka and Santa Fe has laid rails to Dodge City, that this should be a cattle market. Interesting."

"I don't see why not."

They were interrupted by the waitress. Lucina ordered beefsteak, the same thing Will was having. "Do go on with your meal, Will. Please."

Picking up his knife, he cut off a piece of steak and resumed eating. While he ate, she stared into empty space over his head and said, "Hmm. That is something to think about."

He finished his meal but didn't know how to excuse himself, so he drank coffee while she ate. She chewed slowly and silently, seeming to be deep in thought. Then she swallowed and said, "You've noticed that there are no cattle pens here."

"I haven't looked all over, but no, I haven't seen any."

"And no railcars for cattle." Cocking her head to one side, she added, "You have to have a buyer, either at this end or the other end. Where are you planning to ship your cattle? Kansas City?"

"More'n likely. Wichita, maybe."

"So you have a lot of arrangements to make. Tell me, Will, have you had any experience dealing with the railroad?"

"No."

"Neither have I, but I know something about business transactions. Maybe I can help."

"You?"

Her eyes suddenly fixed on his. "Yes, me. A mere woman. Does that surprise you?"

"Well, uh . . ." He didn't know what to say.

"It does surprise you." It was an accusation.

Squirming a little, Will felt his face getting red again. He just didn't know what to say.

"Do you mind if I try?"

51

"Well, uh, no. But why should you?"

"I owe you. You probably saved my life."

"Naw. You don't owe me anything."

She was looking into his eyes again, but thoughtfully, not accusingly. Her dinner was forgotten. He didn't want to get into a staring match with her, so he looked down. Then, "How long are you planning to stay in Dodge City, Will?"

"No longer'n I have to. I've got to get back to the Pease River. My uncle and a dozen cowboys are waitin' for me."

"Then what?"

Damn, she was asking a lot of questions. "Then what? Depends on whether we can ship those cattle from here."

"If you can, you'll be back with the cattle?"

"Yeah, sure."

"Hmm."

"Does that 'Hmm' mean something?"

"I'm thinking." Suddenly, she smiled again. "I'm sorry, Will. Are you having dessert?"

He read the handwritten menu over a row of coffee cups behind a long counter. "Cherry pie. That's for me."

"Me too. Let's chow down, or whatever you cowboys say."

"Chow down? I never heard that before."

"What do you cowboys say?"

Another crooked grin turned up one corner of his mouth. "You don't want to hear it."

A ruckus on Trail Street awakened Lucina at dawn. Men were yelling and horses were trotting up and down on the hard-packed dirt. Wagons were rattling past her second-floor window. For a moment she wondered what was happening, but only for a moment. The soft bed felt so good and she was so tired that she shifted positions and went back to sleep.

She slept on her side with her knees drawn up. And she dreamed of a young man with a crooked nose wearing a wide-brimmed Stetson, boots, and spurs. When she awakened again and realized what she had been dreaming about, she frowned at herself. It wasn't just the dream, it was also her mother's words coming back to her:

"You are past the age where you should let some of the fine young men come calling. You don't want to stay unmarried too long. People will think you are abnormal. Don't you want to be married?"

Abnormal? Yes, definitely, in some ways. But not in all ways. Of course she had given some thought to young men. Of course she had wondered with it was like to, well, to conceive babies. She had dreamed about it. Numerous times. And now she was dreaming about . . .

"Aw hell, goddam," she muttered as she swung her feet out of the bed. "Damnation. Phooey and hell." Those were words she would never use except when she was talking to herself. "The whole world can just go and give itself an enema." Angry with herself as much as anything else, she started to put on a pair of corduroy pants, then changed her mind. "I'm a woman and that is nothing to be ashamed of. If anyone doesn't like it they can just go to hell's fire."

When she tightened the petticoat around her waist, she swore again and wondered why women couldn't be comfortable like men. Finally, washed, combed, and dressed in a blue cotton dress, she was ready to meet the world. At the door she jerked it open, stopped. What was she mad about? The unsuccessful trip out on the prairie? That certainly didn't help. Will Porter and the way he had invited himself into her dream? No, he didn't invite himself. No reason to be mad at him. Oh well.

"Smile," her mother had often said. "It never hurts to

53

smile." Her mother wasn't always wrong. Lucina forced herself to smile and walk down the stairs like a lady.

Trail Street was quiet now. The saloons and bawdy houses didn't get busy until late afternoon. The more buffalo hunters there were in town, the louder the street got. It wasn't unusual to hear shots fired. But Lucina had heard about Abilene and Wichita, and she knew that if Dodge City ever got to be a major shipping point for Texas cattle, it would get louder and wilder.

Her first stop after breakfast was the railroad depot, the short, squat building next to the warehouses. Inside, she approached a long counter and cleared her throat to get the attention of a tall, thin man sitting before a telegraph key on a desk. "Uhumm."

He looked up from under a green eyeshade and stood. "Yes, ma'am."

"Sir, would you be so kind as to tell me the name of the superintendent and where I can reach him?"

"The superintendent? Why in the world . . . ?"

She fixed a stern expression on her face. "Yes, the superintendent. I may have a business proposition for him."

"A business proposition?"

"Yes." And then she remembered her mother's advice, and she forced a small smile. "If you don't mind, sir."

"Huh? Oh. Yeah, yes. Shore. I got a letter from him just a week ago. His address was on it. Just a minute, ma'am, and I'll find it." He turned to the desk, opened a top drawer, and rummaged through it. Failing to find what he was looking for, he shut it and opened the next drawer down. Extracting a sheet of paper, he glanced at it and brought it to her. "His name and address is here at the top of this paper, ma'am. You can write it down if you want to."

The small silk purse she carried contained a dainty handkerchief, some money, a pencil, and pad of paper.

54

She copied the name and address, thanked the stationmaster, and went back to her hotel room. There she found some envelopes and stationery in her luggage—not the dainty, feminine kind, but the no-nonsense type that her father used. Sitting at a small table, she addressed the envelope:

Mr. Hiram Littleton
The Atchison, Topeka and Santa Fe Rail Co.
Post Office Box 449
Kansas City, Missouri

That done, she began to write:

Mr. Hiram Littleton
Dear Sir
    Please allow me to introduce myself: I am Lucina Mays, daughter of Mr. Woodrow H. Mays of Mays Mercantile, and granddaughter of Mr. William L. Rathman of Rathman Wholesale Groceries. My purpose for writing to you is . . ."

She wrote in a neat feminine, wishing it looked masculine. When she finished, she sealed the envelope and went to the post office. But she didn't mail it. While she was walking to the post office, she had done some calculating:

The letter would go out on the eastbound that night and would arrive in Kansas City the next night. It would take the post office a day to sort the mail and another day to deliver it. That was three days. If Mr. Littleton replied instantly, it would be another three days at least before she got an answer. Better figure on a week. Perhaps longer. Would Will Porter stay in Dodge City a week? Probably not. He was anxious to conclude his business here and go back to his cattle.

When he discovered there were no cattle pens anywhere near the railroad and no railcars for cattle, he would go back and his cowboys would drive the herd to Wichita or Ellsworth. She would never see him again.

But that wasn't important, she said under her breath. Not at all. What was important was doing business. She wanted to be a businesswoman. Here was her chance.

She wouldn't mail the letter. She'd go to Kansas City and see Mr. Littleton in person. That would be quicker and much more effective.

For a man, anyway. A woman?

Will Porter soon realized he'd made a long ride for nothing. Five days to Dodge City and five days back. He'd asked everyone he could think of to ask. Hell, the nearest corrals were on a farm owned by some easterners about eight miles north of Dodge City. He'd been to the railroad depot and asked the stationmaster. There were no stock cars anywhere. He'd sent a telegraph to Mr. Littleton at Kansas City, but he wasn't optimistic. The railroad was busy hauling buffalo hides and buffalo meat to the East. It didn't need the cattle business.

Well, he'd wait for an answer to his wire. He couldn't leave without trying. But it sure as hell looked like the Double O outfit was going to have to drive its cattle to Wichita.

Just to have something to do while he waited, he stepped inside the Longbranch Saloon, stood at the bar, and ordered a glass of beer. Only a few men at the table in back and only two others were drinking at the bar.

"You're the gent that sent all them boys down to Adobe Walls, ain't you?" It was the bartender speaking, a handsome man with a handlebar mustache and dark hair parted in the middle.

"Yeah, I saw 'em leavin'. They had enough guns to fight off an army and some wagons fortified with

56

big timbers."

"Why didn't you go with them?" The handsome face wasn't friendly.

"I asked 'em if they needed me, and they said they didn't. I've got to take care of some business here and get back to Texas. Besides," he tried a friendly grin, "I've seen all the Indians I care to see."

"You from Texas?"

The question came from his right. Will half turned and found himself face to face with a husky man who wore a broad-brimmed hat, denim pants, and jackboots. His face was square and hard, and he had a slightly flattened nose. He looked like a bulldog with a hat on.

"Why, yeah," Will said, still trying to be affable.

"You're a cattleman." An accusation.

"Yep, that's what I am."

"You wouldn't be thinkin' about drivin' a bunch of them Texas cattle up here, would you?"

"We're thinkin' about it, yeah."

"Well, you can damn well forget it."

"What? Why?" This was getting serious.

"'Cause we ain't allowin' none of them Texas chiggers or ticks or whatever the hell they are comin' up here and killin' our cattle."

"Your cattle?"

"Yeah. We're runnin' seven hundred good Durham cows and calves north of here, and we ain't gonna allow none of that goddamned Texas fever."

Will shook his head. "We don't have any sick cattle."

"Huh." The husky man snorted. "Them sacks of bones you call cattle don't git sick, but they're bringin' their fever up here and killin' good stock."

"Well, as I understand it, there's no quarantine this far west."

"There ain't yet, but there's gonna be." The man had his hand on the walnut grips of a six-shooter. It was in a holster low on his right hip.

57

Will's mind went to his Smith & Wesson Russian .44 with its ivory grips sticking out of its high Slim Jim holster. The holster was designed to hold the gun in place even when the wearer was on a pitching horse. It was not made for a fast draw. He didn't want to get into a shooting match, anyhow. He kept his hand away from the gun, but his face had turned just as hard as the husky man's face.

He said, "We don't want any trouble, but if we can get the stock cars and all, we're gonna ship some Texas cattle from here."

"Then there's gonna be some shootin'."

"We've been shot at before."

"Then, by God, it's war."

Chapter Eight

Will Porter said no more. He turned his back to the man with the bulldog face and slowly finished his beer. Then he wiped his mouth with a shirtsleeve, turned, and walked out. The spurs on his boots chinged. Every man in the Longbranch Saloon watched him go, and he could feel their eyes on his back. Though his feet wanted to hurry, he forced himself to walk casually. Outside, he paused, tilted his hat brim low to keep the hot Kansas sun out of his face, and wondered what to do next.

It was too early to have received an answer to his telegraph. That would come late in the day if it came at all. He'd already had a bath and a shave. He could use some clean clothes, but he didn't want to spend too much money. What to do? His brown horse needed all the rest it could get, so he left it at the livery pens and walked.

He walked aimlessly, too restless to go back to his hotel and not wanting to get into another argument in a saloon. At the end of Trail Street, he turned and walked back. When he reached the plank sidewalk he met Lucina Mays. She was easily the prettiest girl he had seen in a long time. She smiled. His face split into a broad grin.

"Hello, Miss Mays."

"Hello yourself, Will. I'm Lu, remember?"

"Oh, sure." He stopped, hooked his thumbs in his gunbelt, and faced her. "Are you goin' back to Kansas City?"

"Yes. On the next train east. But I'll return."

"You're comin' back here?"

"Yep. I've got business here."

"What is your business?" He expected her to refuse to answer, but she fooled him.

"That is something I would like to talk to you about. Have you had lunch?"

"Lunch?"

"Dinner, to a Texan, I think."

"Oh. No, not yet."

"Good. Would you care to accompany me to the Dodge House. That's where the best restaurant in town is."

"Fine."

They walked side by side. He started out walking slowly, but soon discovered that she could walk as fast as he could in his boots and spurs. By the time they climbed the porch at the Dodge House, he was wishing she would slow down. The doors and windows of the restaurant were open to let in the prairie breeze. Flies were everywhere. And there was the stink from the mountain of buffalo hides down the street.

"Cattle have to smell better than that," Lucina said, wrinkling her nose as they sat at a table in the dining room.

"Anything smells better than that."

"You haven't found any cattle cars, have you?"

"Naw. No pens, no nothin'."

"It's those hides. And buffalo meat."

"How's that?"

"I did some asking. Will, they have shipped as many as forty thousand hides a month from Dodge City. That's worth about one hundred and twenty thousand dollars."

60

"Good Lord."

"That's why the railroad hasn't even thought of shipping cattle."

"I can believe it."

"Well, I'm going to try to help you. That's why I'm going back to Kansas City."

"You? Help?" When her lips clamped tight he wished he hadn't said that.

"Let me ask you something, Will: What have you done to improve your situation?"

"Done? Well, I sent a telegraph to the railroad superintendent, a man name of Littleton."

"You sent a telegraph. Wonderful. What do you think that will get you?"

Her sarcasm riled him a little. "It'll find out if any cattle cars are available, that's what it'll get me."

"I'll make a bet with you. I'll bet there are no cattle cars available."

"Huh. The odds are on your side."

"All right." Her face had softened now, and a small smile appeared. "I'll offer you another wager. I'll wager I can make some cattle cars available."

"You? How?"

"Wanta bet?"

He had to think about that a moment. "You're sure of yourself, ain't you?"

"No." The smile disappeared. The hazel eyes were serious. "I'm not sure of myself, but I'm willing to take a small gamble. Are you willing to gamble a few days?"

"Why? How?"

"Instead of sending a telegram or writing a letter, I'm going to go see Mr. Littleton."

"Then what?"

Conversation ceased when the waitress appeared. They both ordered a big slice of cherry pie. Lucina looked down at the table a moment, and when she looked up a frown wrinkled her forehead. "I'm gambling two long trips in a passenger coach and I'm

61

taking a chance of making a fool of myself. Will you take a chance and wait until I get back?"

"Why are you doin' it? What's it to you?"

"I'll make a deal with you. How many cattle did you say you have?"

"Well, we lost a few swimmin' the rivers, but we've still got two thousand and eight hundred head."

"If I can arrange for some cattle cars and pens at the railroad, would you pay me a nickel a head? That would be a hundred and forty dollars."

"That's more money than a cowboy makes in four months."

"But I'm taking a gamble. And it would be worth much more than that to you."

He had to grin and shake his head. "I can see how some folks get rich."

"Do we have a deal?"

"Well, I don't think you can do it, but I'll wait three days."

"Four days. Three will probably be enough, but it might not. Can you wait four days."

"I guess so."

"Shake on it?" She held out her right hand.

Thinking he might be making a mistake, he took her hand.

The westbound train came in late that afternoon, went on past Dodge City a ways, and turned around on a loop in the tracks. Leaning against a warehouse wall, Will watched men load the buffalo hides, while the steam engine hissed, groaned, and belched fire like a huge dragon. Will had read about the dragons back in the days of the knights in armor, and he could easily imagine the string of cars behind the engine being a dragon's tail. It was one hell of a big brute and a powerful one. He could picture what it would do if it got loose and went wild. It would flatten the whole town and eat everybody in it. Those buffalo guns would only make it angrier. Will ran it through his mind and grinned at himself. Yes sir, there was one brute he wouldn't want to tangle with.

Eventually he got bored with watching other men work, and walked back toward the hotel. It would probably take most of the night to load those hides. He had supper alone, wondering where Lucina Mays was keeping herself, then drifted back onto the street. The pile of buffalo hides had disappeared, and doors were being slammed shut on the railcars. The steam engine whistled loud enough to be heard clear down on the Canadian, was still a minute, and then whistled again. People appeared on a wooden platform in front of the depot, well-dressed people. Among them was Lucina Mays, carrying a leather suitcase. Will ambled over.

"Wish me luck, Will."

"I do, Miss Mays. Good luck to you. Can I carry this?" He reached for the suitcase.

"No thank you. I can carry it." Damn, she was pretty. And determined. Will could see that in the set of her jaw.

The passengers were stepping up onto a low stool and climbing into a chair car, a passenger coach. Lucina followed them. "Wait for me, Will."

"I'll keep my end of the bargain."

"That's all I ask." She disappeared inside.

The hissing engine whistled again. A man in a striped cap and bib overalls leaned out of the cab window and pulled a chain that brought another whistle. He did it twice. Two minutes later the engine moved. The first car jerked, sending a series of jerks down the line of cars. The engine belched fire, blew steam, and spun its wheels. Slowly, the train got moving.

On his way back to the hotel, Will stopped in a mercantile and bought a paperback book that was published in New York City. In his room, he lay on the bed with his head propped up on a pillow and read

63

about wild Indians and cowboys away Out West.

It was a bone-weary young woman who walked stiffly through Kansas City's Union Station. No bed on the western prairie was as uncomfortable as that bench-of-a-seat on the passenger coach. She had sat on it all night and all day, and when she thought Kansas City was only a few more hours away the train had come to a stop. She heard men outside yelling up and down the track, but never did know what was wrong. The conductor said only that there would be a small delay. They stayed there most of the night. Now, early in the morning, the station was a busy place, with passengers in a hurry to go elsewhere.

Lucina carried her one piece of luggage outside to a hansom cab pulled by a black horse. She climbed inside and settled back against the padded seat. Too tired to watch the city go by, she closed her eyes and listened to the clip-clop of the horse's hooves on the brick streets. Finally, a "Whoa," and she was there. The two-story white frame house with its wide porch, expansive green lawn, and two big oak trees was home.

Her father and brothers were at their offices this time of morning, and no one greeted her. Still, her spirits picked up a notch when she walked up the flagstone path and stepped onto the porch. She knew who would open the door. And sure enough, when she tapped the door with the brass door-knocker, it was Grumps, as Lucina had always called her.

The old woman looked the same, in her long shapeless dress and her gray hair tied in a bun at the back of her head. A few tendrils hung over her ears. She wore the usual grumpy expression.

But when she Lucina, the wrinkled face split into a wide smile. "Lucina. Come in, child. It's so good to see you. Come in, child, come in this house." And she

64

turned her head and yelled, "Miz Mays, it's Lucina. It's Lucina, Miz Mays. She's home."

And her mother appeared from the parlor, paused a moment at the hallway, then came on, walking faster with arms outstretched. "Oh, thank heavens, Lucina, thank heavens." Then they were in each other's arms, hugging, her mother crying. "Lucina we were so worried. Thank heavens you're back. Let me look at you, Lucina."

Mrs. Mays stepped back. Her wet gray eyes with a worry frown between them went over her daughter carefully. She was in her fifties, but a handsome woman with a slender figure and hair carefully coiffured. "Are you well? How do you feel? You must be terribly tired."

"I'm just fine, Mother. I am a little tired, but I can't rest yet."

"What on earth do you mean?"

"I have something to do. I must take a bath and put on some clean clothes and go back to the Union Station."

"What on earth for?"

"Business. I have some business to take care of and it won't wait."

"Lucina, what . . . ?"

"I'll be back for dinner, Mother, then I have things to tell all of you, and, boy oh boy is my bed going to feel good."

Her mother left her her privacy while she bathed in the tin bathtub in the water closet, but not while she brushed her hair and dressed. "Lucina, why are you so secretive? What is this business you have to take care of? Talk to your mother, young lady."

"I will Mother. Honest. It's just that right now, I have something very important to take care of. It's something that I have to do and I have to do it exactly right." She picked her most businesslike outfit, a dark

65

blue broadcloth skirt with a white ruffled blouse. The string of pearls her father had given her for a birthday present would look good.

No. No jewelry.

She practiced fixing a businesslike, no-nonsense expression on her face. Damn, she wished her mother would quit talking so she could concentrate.

But she didn't say anything. Instead, before she left, she hugged her mother again and said, "This is very important. Would you wish me luck, Mother?"

"Of course. Whatever it is you are doing, it's obviously important to you, and yes, I do wish you luck."

Carrying a small leather case with her notebook, figures, and a man-sized pen, she walked two blocks to an intersection where she hoped an empty cab would come by. Luck was with her. A hansom was waiting, one horse standing with its head down, asleep on its feet. The cabby was sitting on his high seat reading a newspaper. "Union Station," Lucina said. On the way, she rehearsed what she was planning to say.

Mr. Littleton was in, but he had a luncheon appointment and could spare no time. Would the young lady care to come back later?

Lucina made a decision. All right, so she wasn't going to do this entirely on her own. A businesswoman would be a fool not to take every advantage she could. "I am Lucina Mays," she told the secretary, standing across a mahogany desk from her. "My father is Woodrow H. Mays of Mays Mercantile, and my grandfather is William L. Rathman of Rathman Wholesale Groceries. I have a business proposition which I am sure will interest Mr. Littleton."

After considering that a moment, the secretary, a middle-aged, well-groomed woman, said, "Very well. I will tell Mr. Littleton you are here." She stood, opened a door with a frosted pane, and went inside. The sign painted in black script letters on the door pane read:

Mr. Hiram Littleton
Superintendent Western Division
Atchison, Topeka and Santa Fe Railway Co.

Lucina was too nervous to sit. She had to compose herself. Clearing her throat, she went over it again quietly. "Mr. Littleton, I have just returned from Dodge City, and I have some facts and figures here that are of great importance to the railway company. If you will permit me, sir . . ." Oh God, could she do it?

The office door opened. Lucina was beckoned inside.

Chapter Nine

How could he have been so dumb? The more Will Porter thought about it, the dumber he felt. Let a girl talk him into hanging around Dodge City for four days. A damned girl. Strange, mysterious. All right, she was pretty and she seemed to have a lot more sense than most women, but a girl just the same.

How was he going to explain this to Lucas? He'd never live it down. Never mind that she'd helped him fight off Indians. Never mind that she had serious hazel eyes that could make a man believe anything. All they would know is he let a girl talk him into wasting four days.

Well, at least he'd earned a little more respect in Dodge City. All those heavily armed men who'd headed for Adobe Walls were back now with a couple of survivors. The story was being told over and over. Seemed the day after Will left, two men arrived at Adobe Walls in a wagon pulled by two horses, and the next day more buffalo hunters arrived. By the time the rescue group got started, about a hundred hunters had gathered at Adobe Walls, and there wasn't an Indian in sight. The would-be rescuers had met two surviving hunters coming toward Dodge City, and when they heard that all was well, they came back.

The two hunters recognized Will and insisted on

buying him a drink of whiskey in the Longbranch. The bartender with the handlebar mustache and slicked-back hair was treating Will with more respect now. But Will was not a heavy drinker, and after buying a round for the two hunters, he said he had a horse to look after and got outside.

It was two days ago that Lucina Mays had left. No answer to the telegraph he'd sent to Hiram Littleton. Hell. Well, he'd promised he'd wait four days, and he'd keep his word. Dammit.

Back in his room he read a while, put the book down, and chuckled. Those New York writers had a hell of an imagination, but what they wrote about was a picnic compared to the battle at Adobe Walls. Wait until word of the battle got to New York. That would give them something to write. It would be interesting to see what they had to say about it, and how many different ways the story would be told.

Getting more bored by the hour, he went back to the Longbranch. The beer was warm and not very good, so when he finished that he ordered a shot of whiskey. It wasn't very good either. He took a couple of small sips, then decided to knock it back and get it over with. Gaw-ud. He nearly strangled.

Outside on the plank sidewalk, he realized the whiskey had gone to his head. Some whiskey. Must have been the rottenest stuff ever bottled. He had to walk carefully to keep from staggering. Uh-oh. "Excuse me, mister."

"Excuse you, hell. Who the hell do you think you are?"

Through bleary eyes, Will appraised the man. Aw hell, wouldn't you know it, the man had a star pinned to his vest. "I didn't mean to bump you. Excuse me."

"You're that goddam Texas cowboy I've been hearing about, ain't you?"

Now that he was thinking about it, he hadn't bumped the man, the man had bumped him. "Yeah."

His vision was clearing now.

"And I reckon you think you're gonna take over Dodge City."

"Take over? Why no."

"The hell you ain't. I seen it before. I was deputy marshal at Abilene when you goddam Texans thought you could just take over and do as you damned well pleased. Well, I'm the marshal here, and I know all about your kind, and I'm telling you right now, you ain't taking over Dodge."

"All we want to do is ship some cattle from here."

"Hah. If I let you do that there'll be more cattle and more of you goddam troublemaking cowboys, and I by God ain't gonna allow it."

"I've never heard of any law against it."

The lawman was buggy-whip thin, but he looked to be as tough as a boot. He wore a cattleman's hat, a gray shirt with a black wool vest, and black wool pants. He carried a six-gun in a cutaway holster low on his right hip, and his right hand stayed near it. His black boots were the low-heeled kind that mule skinners wore.

"I'm the goddam law." The words came from under a brown, bushy mustache. "I was hired to keep the peace in this town, and I'm by God gonna keep the peace. If I see more than two of you goddam cowboys together I'm gonna lock you all up."

At first Will wanted to shrug it off and go on about his business. He hadn't violated any law and he had done nothing to provoke a fight. Just shrug it off and forget it. But this man was serious. He had a badge and he had authority and he intended to show him who was boss. Will felt anger rising in his throat. Still, he didn't want a fight. He tried to go around him.

The marshal sidestepped to block his way. "Do you hear what I'm saying?"

"Yeah." The anger was ready to explode, and Will hissed through his teeth. "I hear you, and now you listen to me, we're gonna bring a herd of cattle up here

70

and unless you've got a law to show us you ain't gonna stop us."

"Maybe I ought to lock you up right now. Teach you some respect for the law."

Will faced the marshal squarely, his right thumb hooked in his gunbelt directly over the butt of his Russian .44. His eyes were locked on the marshal's eyes. "Try it."

They faced each other, each daring the other to move. Will knew he could die right here, and the marshal could say he started the fight. The marshal could kill him and get by with it because he was a lawman. Will didn't want to die. But he wasn't going to back down from this sonofabitch either.

They faced each other. One of them was going to have to do something.

And suddenly the tension was broken.

"My goodness, marshal, can't a body go on about her business without you men blocking the sidewalk?" She was middle aged, in a long dark dress and a poke bonnet. She had come up behind the marshal. Her face wore a stern expression and her eyes were punishing.

"Oh, uh, excuse me, ma'am." The marshal touched his hat brim and stepped aside. "I didn't mean to block your way."

Will stepped aside, too.

"One would think," the woman scolded, "that you would have more respect for the citizens who pay you." She went on.

The men stood awkwardly, not knowing what to do. Finally, the marshal spoke, "You keep in mind what I said." He turned on his heels and left.

"Yeah," Will said to his back, "I'll keep you in mind, all right."

For a long moment he stayed where he was and watched the marshal walk away. "Gaw-ud damn," he muttered to himself. "We ain't even come near here with any cattle yet and already two men have tried to

71

pick a fight with me. If we bring that herd up here there'll more'n likely be some shootin'—and some dyin'.

"But if we can get the railcars, we're damned sure gonna bring 'em up here."

The third day was the longest day. He didn't dare go into a saloon and drink. Seemed there were too many men around town who wanted to pick a fight. That wouldn't do. He had other things on his mind, like getting back to the Pease River, his uncle Lucas, and a herd of cattle. All he could do was walk, read, and wait.

He was listening for the train whistle, and heard it long before it got to town. She'd said four days, and she couldn't be on this train, but he had nothing else to do so he ambled over to the depot to see who got off.

The big engine chug-chugged, hissed, and puffed on past the depot. Then brakes screeched and drive wheels spun backward as the train came to a stop with the passenger car in front of the wooden platform. Leaning against the depot, Will watched passengers climb stiffly out. There were two men, one in a business suit and the other in overalls. Then a young woman.

It was her.

Standing straight now, Will sighed with relief. Finally his wait was over. Weariness was etched on her face, and her clothes were wrinkled, but still she was a very pretty young woman. When she saw Will she smiled.

"Howdy, Miss Mays. Glad to see you back."

"Hello, Will. Yes, I'm back and I've got news."

He reached for her suitcase, but she drew it away from him. "Good news or bad?" he asked.

"Good news. We'll get the cattle cars."

"Huh? You jokin'?"

"No, I'm not joking. I'll tell you all about it, but can I

72

freshen up first? Can we meet in the hotel dining room?"

"Sure, but . . ."

"I'm starved, and that coach car is about as comfortable as a brick street. I won't be long. Will you wait?"

A slow grin turned up one side of his mouth. "Well, I've been doin' nothin' but waitin'. I reckon a few more minutes won't matter. I can't leave 'till mornin' anyhow."

They walked. As tired as she was, she didn't walk so fast. Again he reached for her suitcase, and was surprised when she surrendered it. At the Dodge House, he carried it up the stairs for her. With spurs on his boots he had to turn his feet sideways to walk back down the stairs. In the hotel dining room he sat at a table and drank coffee. A feller would think, after waiting three days, that a few more minutes would be easy. But damn he wished she'd hurry. Then she appeared in the doorway.

Standing, he started to pull out a chair for her, but she beat him to it. "Just coffee for the moment," she said to the waitress. "We'll have dinner later." The coffee was poured in a china cup. Folding her arms on top of the table, she leaned forward, and asked, "How long will it take to drive all those cattle up here, Will?"

He drawled, "Well, let's see, it'll take me five days ridin' to get back to the Pease, and we can move cattle at about a third of that speed. It'll take, oh, twenty or twenty-five days."

A frown wrinkled her forehead. "That soon?"

"Why?"

"I have a commitment from Mr. Littleton to send some cattle cars to Dodge City and to build some cattle pens at the railroad. But it may take a little longer than that."

"You really did get a promise?"

73

"Yes."

"How'd you do that?"

"I, uh, I just laid some facts before him. He is not stupid. He realized that what I had to say was correct."

"What kind of facts?"

She spread her hands, then crossed her arms again. "I'm looking for a business opportunity, and I'm always keeping my ears and eyes open and listening. Too, I ask questions. What I've learned is, well, something that Mr. Littleton hadn't thought about. But when I presented my case, he did think about it and he is smart enough to make a decision."

"Your case?"

"Yes. It's really simple. Look at it this way, Will. Dodge City was founded to cater to the buffalo hunters. The railroad laid track here to haul buffalo hides and buffalo met to the East, and to haul supplies out West. It has been very profitable to everyone concerned. But . . ." Again, she spread her hands. "The buffalo are nearly gone from Kansas. The hunters are moving south. My gosh, Will, they've been killing the animals by the thousands. There is not an unlimited supply. Every merchant in town is worried. Business is moving away.

"But"—Lucina Mays leaned farther across the table—"then you came along. Do you see what I'm driving at?"

"Uh-huh." He grinned a small grin. "So all you had to do was tell Hiram Littleton about all this."

"Exactly. And there is something else. That quarantine. Cattlemen have found a way to get around it, but the homesteaders, the farmers, are moving west, and they are getting fighting mad about Texas cattle bringing Texas fever to Kansas. That quarantine line is moving west with the settlers. Fortunately, it hadn't reached his far west, and probably it never will."

"Uh-huh. I, my uncle and I, have done some thinking about that."

74

"But Mr. Littleton was not thinking about it. Now, he is. That was another selling point."

Draining his coffee cup, Will ran it all through his mind. Lucina Mays talked on:

"Among the other things I have learned is this: Abilene lost the cattle business when the railroad got to Wichita. Wichita is closer to Texas. It was a hard economic blow, so hard that the town fathers paid men to meet the trail herds and talk them into going to Abilene. They promised all kinds of things." She took another sip of coffee. "I reminded Mr. Littleton of that too. The cattle business has been and still is very important to the economics of Kansas and especially to the railroads."

Will had to admire her. "Boy, if that didn't convince him nothin' could."

Suddenly, her shoulders slumped and her face turned sour. "I wish I could take all the credit, but I had to have some help."

"How come?"

"Perhaps you haven't noticed it, Will, but I am a woman. And if that weren't problem enough, I am a young woman."

At that, he had to laugh. "You think I haven't noticed? Every man in this town has noticed."

"It isn't funny. No matter how much business sense I made, Mr. Littleton had to contact my grandfather before he would take me seriously."

"Oh." Will understood.

"My grandfather Rathman founded and owns Rathman Wholesale Groceries and he does a lot of business with the railroads. When he talks, people listen."

All Will could do was look down at his hands on top of the table. When he looked up he said, "I can understand how it is—no, I take that back, I don't understand how it is to be a girl—but I can imagine how it is to . . . what I mean is, you think of things that

75

most folks don't think of and you make a lot of sense. Bein' a girl—woman—shouldn't matter."

She put her hands on top of his and smiled again. "You're a good fellow, Will."

Sure, but after dinner, after she'd gone to her room, he was glad that her grandfather was in on it. That Hiram Littleton didn't make a promise just to get some girl out of his office, he'd made a promise to an important businessman, the kind of man he wouldn't lie to. As much as he liked and admired Lucina Mays, Will had to admit to himself that that made him feel better.

And next morning, as he headed southwest, traveling light, with two blankets and a bare five days of grub on the back of his saddle, he felt good about his mission to Dodge City. It was a success, and there was no doubt he had to thank Lucina Mays and her business mind for that. He would tell his uncle Lucas about her.

He would have to tell also about a Durham farmer who'd threatened war and a town marshal who hated Texas cowboys. Their troubles weren't over.

Chapter Ten

A tired cowboy and a leg-weary horse finally topped a brown, grassy hill deep into Texas and saw the Pease River below. "Can't be far now, feller," Will Porter said to the horse. They went down the hill at a trot, and the cowboy mused, "No rain at all. There's nothin' green in sight." Two miles west, they topped another hill. There they stopped and the cowboy stood in his stirrups, waved his hat and yelled:

"Hyo-o-o."

They were down there, twenty-eight hundred head of cattle, grazing on the brown grass. A few cowboys were riding among them, the chuck wagon was parked near the river, and the remuda grazed a mile away. Old Jim, the gray-haired, stiff-legged wrangler, sat on the ground in the shade of his horse and watched the remuda.

"Hyo-o-o. Hey, you knotheads."

The two cowboys nearest Will stopped and stared a moment. Then they came toward him at a gallop. He booted the brown horse into a lope. When they met at the bottom of the hill, they all stopped and grinned at each other.

Then a cowboy named Clint Overhart stopped grinning, turned to the other with a serious face, and said, "This cain't be the Porter boy."

77

"Naw," said the other, also serious now.

"Does look kinda like 'im."

"Dunno. Ain't seen 'im for so long I forgot what he looks like."

Will glanced from one to the other while they talked.

"Same clothes, same hat. Got a hole in it, howesomever."

"I recognize that brown hoss."

"Wal, if it looks like 'im, and it's wearin' his clothes and ridin' his hoss, it must be him."

The wide grins returned.

"Will, you goddam cocklebur, how come you're still alive?"

"Yeah, we thought old Quanah had your hair a-hangin' from his teepee."

Grinning, Will said, "Old Quanah is lucky he's got his head. Where's Lucas?"

"Yonder, lookin' at the cattle. He looks 'em all over ever' day and adds up the pounds."

"He's been worried sick about you, Will. He don't say nothin' but he's worried. You better go over and say howdy to 'im before he has a shit hemorrhage."

His uncle didn't see him until he was only fifty feet away, and then his eyes and his face didn't change expressions. He looked older to Will, a little rounded in the shoulders, slumped in the saddle.

"Evenin', Lucas." Will reined up beside Lucas Porter's sorrel horse.

"Evenin', Will." The older man still didn't change expressions. A three-day growth of gray whiskers covered the bottom half of his leathery face. "How's things up in Kansas?"

"I was promised some cattle cars on the Atchison, Topeka and Santa Fe. There's none there now, but I was promised some."

"That's where we'll go then."

Will thought he ought to apologize for being gone so long, and he said, "Got in an Indian fight at Adobe

Walls, and when I got to Dodge City I had to wait a few days to find out if we could get some cars."

Both horses were stamping their feet and switching their tails against the flies. Lucas Porter looked at the western horizon from under his wide hat brim. "Don't matter. We're in no hurry. These beefs put on a few pounds here. When did you eat last?"

"I ran out of chuck last night."

"Go on over to the wagon and tell ol' China Eye to find somethin' for you to eat. He won't feed the boys 'till after sundown, but he can find somethin' for you."

"Yeah." He thought of telling his uncle how happy he was to see him, but the older Porter always kept his emotions to himself and wanted everyone else to do the same. He turned his horse around.

"Will."

He stopped, looked back.

"You ain't hurt or nothin'?"

He grinned. "Naw."

The cowboy crew was in good spirits when Lucas Porter announced that first thing in the morning they would gather the cattle and get them strung out, headed for Dodge City. It had been boring. The cattle were easy to handle and it didn't take much riding to keep them from straying too far.

But first, after the cook had taken all his pots, dutch ovens, and buckets out of the supper fire, they sat on their canvas-wrapped beds near it and insisted that Will tell them every detail of the battle at Adobe Walls.

"Yeah, son," said China Eye, so named because his left eye was milky white and sightless, "a buffler hunter came by a week or so ago and told us about it. Said there was a young cattleman that stopped there for the night and got caught up in the shootin'. Said you was the only one that had a hoss when the shootin' was over and you took off on a high lope for Dodge City. Didn't know if you got there."

"I got there." Will stared into the fire. "Met a, uh,

boy on the way and the two of us fought off four Indians. Cheyennes, I think." He told all about Adobe Walls, all the details. Men smoked pipes and hand-rolled cigarettes and listened. Lucas Porter listened. Will concluded with: "Those Big Fifty buffalo guns can knock an Indian off a horse a mile away," and he told about the last shot fired in the battle.

"Cain't say I blame the Injuns too much," a cowboy allowed, "but that Quanah is a mean sonofabitch. He'll kill women and babies as quick as he'll kill a man."

"I heered," said another, "their favorite game is to torture prisoners. The louder they can make 'em holler, the more kick they get out of it."

"Like the feller says, if you git in a fight with 'em and cain't win, save the last bullet for yourself."

Then Will told them about the threats from a Durham farmer and a town marshal. "We ain't gonna be greeted like long-lost brothers," he said.

"Tell yuh, boys," China Eye put in. "I been up to Wichita and I been up to Abilene, and some a them Kansas folks hold Texans at a discount. When I heered Will'd stayed alive at Adobe Walls I was worried that some a them corn-fed farmers might a put a load of buckshot in 'im."

"That's the way of it, all right," said Clint Overhart. "Up at Abilene they hired the toughest, meanest sons of bitches they could find to make believers out of us."

"That's a fact," said China Eye. "Shore is."

At midmorning they had the cattle gathered and strung out for a mile or more. The chuck wagon, pulled by two big horses, and the remuda, herded by Jim, followed. They stayed west of the old Chisholm Trail and made their own trail north by northeast. Will was the only man in the crew who had been over that country, and his uncle put him on point. He was one of two point riders, who stayed just a little behind the big steers that were in the lead and kept them going in the right direction. Behind them were the swing riders, who kept the herd from straying too far out of the line; and at the rear, about forty yards behind the stragglers, were the drag riders.

The cattle were mostly three- and four-year-old beeves, and there was little of the bawling that came from cows and calves. They didn't have to be pushed. After being driven up from the Pecos River they were trail broken and went along of their own will. The crew allowed them to graze as they walked, with the goal of traveling about twenty miles a day and getting to Dodge City with healthy cattle. It was an easy job for the cowboys—until they came to the rivers.

The Red River was the first, two-and-a-half days after they'd left the Pease, two days after the cattle and horses had had a taste of water. Lucas Porter went ahead, looking for a place to cross. The damned river had steep banks on each side as far as he could see. When he came back, Will met him and told him about a buffalo trail he remembered crossing on his way back from Kansas. It was about four miles farther west, he believed. Lucas Porter gave his orders to the crew.

Instead of yelling, he pointed in the direction he wanted the herd to go, and Will and the other swing rider booted their horses into a lope to catch up with the leaders and get them turned west. Nobody changed positions with the herd. No cowboy ever rode around another cowboy. That would have been an insult, telling the other man he wasn't doing his job. The boss had to know where each rider was, and changing positions would have made that impossible.

It took another three hours to get within sight of the river, and the cattle smelled water. Knowing that thirst and heat could cause a stampede, Lucas Porter motioned for the drag riders and swing men to crowd the cattle into the river and keep them moving. Besides, it was easier to get cattle across a river at the end of a day than at the beginning. Cowboys pulled off their boots and tied them to saddle horns, loosened their saddle cinches, and urged their horses into the water.

Yelling, swinging lariats, swearing, they pushed and beat cattle into the muddy river. Only about thirty feet of the Red River was swimming deep then, and shortly before dark, all men and animals were across. Half the crew stayed with the herd, got it grazing, and the other half went back for the chuck wagon. They had to get the wagon across. There would be no supper without it.

The harness horses were unhitched and swum across, dragging the double tree and single trees behind them. On the other side, they were hitched to a long half-inch rope tied to the wagon tongue. Men piled their rolled-up beds on top of the load in the wagon, and two men tied long ropes to the front of the wagon and dallied the other ends around their saddle horns. Then, with four men pushing from behind, the wagon was run into the water, and with four horses pulling, it was soon across. Made of wood, the wagon floated, but water came above the floorboards, dampening some of China Eye's groceries.

"You boys ain't gonna have nothin' but your tobacca for supper," he said, but he was joking. Just when the crew was resigned to eating cold, damp biscuits, China Eye uncovered a pot of beef stew, and bellowed, "Git me somethin' to burn and we'll eat." Driftwood was plentiful, and the stew tasted just as good warmed up as it did when it was fresh.

"How many more rivers between here and Dodge City?" The question was directed at Will.

"Oh, there's the Canadian and the Cimarron, and there's the Arkansas runnin' right through the town. Now that we've crossed the Red, we're in the Texas Panhandle. Ain't far to Kansas."

Night horses were roped out of the remuda and tied where they would be handy, and cowboys began taking turns riding night guard. Again, no orders were given. The crew knew what to do.

"How's the grass up there in Kansas?" Lucas Porter

asked his nephew as they rode side by side near the leaders.

"Dry up there too, but now that the buffalo are mostly gone there's plenty of it. Seems to be good feed."

"Did that railroader have any idea when he'd have some cattle cars?"

Will hadn't mentioned Lucina Mays, not sure how his uncle would take it, but he knew he was going to have to. Now was as good a time as any. He half turned in his saddle and faced his uncle.

"I gotta tell you somethin', Lucas, it was a girl who promised the cars." Lucas Porter stared in disbelief at his nephew, but before he could say anything, Will talked on: "She went all the way to Kansas City to explain to the railroad superintendent why we need 'em and to sell 'im on the idea of sending us some. I . . . to tell the truth, I don't think I could have done that. I'm not that good a talker."

Lucas Porter's shaggy eyebrows went up, then down again. "Is she pretty?"

"Yeah, she is. Damned pretty. But she's got a business head on her shoulders."

"Uh-huh."

"It's not what you're thinkin'. She came from a family of businessmen and she sees things the way a businessman sees 'em. If it wasn't for her we'd be goin' all the way to Wichita."

The older Porter was looking at the horizon again, and Will could guess what was going on in his mind. "Tell you the truth, I was kinda leery of her promise myself, but then she said the superintendent made the same promise to her grandpa. Her grandpa is a big businessman in Kansas City, and I don't believe that railroader would lie to him."

"Is that so?" Lucas Porter was still looking at the horizon.

"And like I already said, she didn't promise the cars

would be there when we get there, but she said they wouldn't be too long comin'. And, oh yeah, I made a promise too, I promised we'd pay her a nickel a head if she arranged for the cars and some shippin' pens."

Without turning his head, Lucas Porter drawled, "Wal, I sent you up there to make a decision and you made a decision." He touched spurs to his horse and trotted away, getting ahead of the herd where he could scout the country.

Will watched him go, and muttered to himself, "God oh God, I hope I made the right one."

Chapter Eleven

They'd come from Tennessee, the Porters. When they sold the plantation after the war, Lucas, the older of two brothers, went to Texas, bought land and cattle, and started the Double O outfit. Howard, the younger one, was married and had a son, and wanted an easier life for his family. He stayed in Nashville and bought a cotton gin. But Howard had taken a rifle ball in the right side during the war, and he never fully recovered from it. When his son Horace William Porter was fourteen, he died. The doctor said it was pneumonia, but everyone knew that rifle ball was still in his side and had poisoned him to death. Soon after Howard Porter died, his wife Minnie was killed by a runaway team of horses. Lucas Porter came east to attend both funerals and stayed long enough to sell the cotton gin and put the money in his nephew's name in a Nashville bank. It would be safe there. Then he put a hand on his nephew's shoulder and said:

"You're my boy now, Will. Let's go to Texas."

When Will reached twenty-one he wanted to take his money out of the Nashville bank and buy more land and cattle. His uncle talked him out of it. "Wait a few years," Lucas Porter had said. "Git out in the world and have some experiences, then decide what you want to do."

Will followed his advice. He had to see more of the world than the Double O. His first trip was to Nashville, where he transferred his money to a national bank in San Antonio. Then he went to the Black Mountains of New Mexico and dug for silver. Hell, he didn't know silver from horse manure. Besides, digging in the rocks wasn't his kind of work. Next he went to northern New Mexico and cowboyed on the OT outfit. Six months later he was off to central Arizona to rope wild cattle out of the brushy canyons. He bought the Smith & Wesson Russian .44 from a dried-up old desert rat in Albuquerque. It wasn't a gunfighter's favorite kind of weapon, but he had no intention of being a gunfighter.

In fact, when he got into a barroom brawl in San Francisco, he used his fists. Even when the waterfront tough grabbed for a six-gun, Will punched him hard in the face, knocked him down, and stomped the gun out of his hand.

To hell with San Francisco. What did he go there for, anyway? To see the sights? Well, he'd seen the sights. For a few days he was awed by all the opulence and elegance, but the people were too uppity, phony, dishonest. In Texas a man who wouldn't keep his word had few friends. In San Francisco lying, cheating, double-dealing was a way of life. Then there was the other side of town, where a man's life wasn't worth two-bits. Hell, the Comanches were gentlemen compared to these waterfront thugs. Their favorite weapon was a knife, and they'd cut a man's heart out for the price of a jug of cheap wine. San Francisco could keep its goddam sights.

He'd gathered his two horses from a livery barn and ridden east, back to Texas. Now he knew for sure what he wanted. He wanted good horses and long-horn cattle. He wanted a lot of country around him. It was a long ride back, but he took his time. And on the way he had to smile at the words he'd once heard a cattleman speak:

"If I owned Texas and hell, I'd live in hell and rent out Texas."

But Texas was home.

They crossed the Canadian with little trouble. The river had a reputation for being quicksandy, but it was a dry year and only a few cattle had to be dragged out of the sucking mud. They weren't far from where Will had first seen Lucina Mays. He grinned inwardly when he remembered the way she'd tried to disguise herself.

Some boy.

Two days north of the Canadian they saw Indians. But there were only a half dozen old bucks and a few squaws and big-eyed kids. Lucas Porter signaled for the crew to stay where they were, and he and Will rode over to meet them.

They had four horses, dragging travois, which carried their buffalo-hide shelters. All the Indians were walking. Three of the bucks carried old Civil War Springfield rifles and the others bows and arrows. When they saw the white men riding toward them, they put down their weapons.

"I reckon they're friendly," Lucas Porter said to his nephew, "but you can't be sure. There could be a whole damned army of 'em over that rise there."

"No matter how friendly they look, they hate white eyes."

When they rode closer, the oldest of the bucks, a man with white hair down to his shoulders and a million tiny wrinkles in his round face, held up one hand. He held the hand shoulder high, index and middle fingers together, and raised it level with the top of his head. It meant friend. He wore a white man's lace shoes, white wool pants, and nothing else. The Porters made the same signal. Then the old Indian rubbed his bare stomach.

87

"I don't see no chuck on those travois," Lucas Porter said. "Maybe they're hungry."

The old one rubbed his stomach again and pointed to the sqaws and children.

"I ain't seen a buffalo for a long time," Will allowed. "They're hungry."

"Whatta you think, Will?"

"There's a brindle steer that's lame and has a hard time keepin' up."

"Uh-huh. Let's go back."

The Indians watched as the two cattlemen rode back to their herd and cut out a brindle steer. They drove the limping steer back to where the Indians stood and nodded at the old man. With a wide grin, the Indian picked up his long-barreled Springfield and shot the steer through the heart. It collapsed immediately, and it no more than hit the ground when the squaws were on it with their long knives, skinning and butchering.

"That'll keep 'em eatin' for a while," Will allowed.

"Damn, I do believe they're gonna eat it raw."

Back at the herd, a cowboy said, "They'd cut your throats if they had a chance."

"Yeah," Lucas Porter agreed. "Them shoes he's wearin' had to of come off a dead white man. But the kids . . . I can't stand to see kids go hungry."

It was decision time for Lucina Mays. Will Porter wouldn't be back for at least fifteen days. Should she get on her horse and go south again? She had the supplies she needed, and nobody in Dodge City had seen an unfriendly Indian for weeks.

In her hotel room, she spread the map out on the bed again and for the hundredth time studied it. Drawn with a lead pencil on a piece of wrapping paper, it was simple. Too damned simple. The Cimarron was there and a crooked line ran from northeast to southwest. The words Santa Fe Trail were written along it. A short wavy line was supposed to represent a ravine north of the Cimarron. An arrow pointed northeast, mostly east, and the words Kansas City had been written in a shaky hand. An X marked the important spot.

Trouble was there was too damned much country north of the river and too many ravines.

"Damnation," Lucina muttered. "Hell's fire. I don't give myself a damn how hard it is, I'm not giving up."

But she needed more information to go on. At least one more clue.

Should she load her packhorse and get on her saddle horse and resume her search, or should she go back to Kansas City and question her father and brothers for the hundredth time? They had been to Dodge City, looked, and given up. They had told her all about their trip west and answered her questions over and over. But Grandfather Mays had told them about it, not her, and had drawn the map for them. They shouldn't have given up so easily.

She reached a decision. Rather than wander around by herself in what could be a dangerous territory, she'd go back and question them again. Maybe they'd remember something else that Grandfather Mays had said, something they hadn't mentioned before.

Besides, she wanted to see Hiram Littleton again, remind him of his commitment, keep him honest. Nobody liked pushy people, especially pushy women, but there were times when a body had to do a little pushing.

And if older brother Frank gave her that silly smirk, she'd by gosh haul off and knock it right off his gosh-damned face.

When they crossed the Cimarron they guessed they were in Kansas. It was an easy crossing. Still no rain, and the river wasn't up to its usual strength. On the north bank they made camp and let the cattle scatter

89

and graze. Before sundown they gathered them and held them in a huge bunch about a mile north of the river. Dark clouds were gathering on the western horizon, and Lucas Porter said, "Maybe it'll rain and green things up."

"Right now it's drier'n a popcorn fart," a cowboy commented.

"Uh-oh, see that?" China Eye wiped his hands on a dirty apron and nodded toward the west. "Lightnin'. This country is worse'n Texas, boys. You can be dyin' for rain and all you'll git is the goddam lightnin', and the only thing that's good for is startin' grass fires."

"Dry as this grass is, it'd burn for a hundred miles."

"We'll double the guard tonight," Lucas Porter said, "and keep the cattle close to the river 'till the sky clears. If there's a grass fire on one side of the river we'll go to the other side."

Will was awakened around midnight, and when he pushed the bed tarp off his head he saw the sky was still cloudy. Lightning flashed off to the west. He pulled on his boots and went out to a picket line to find his night horse. As dark as it was he couldn't tell one horse from another until a cowboy asked, "What're you ridin' tonight, Will, old Scrappy?"

"Yeah."

"He's over to your left. I re'clect seein' 'im there."

Will identified the bay horse by groping the saddle on its back. The horse snorted. "Whoa, feller. Whoa now." He tightened the cinches and mounted. "Behave yourself, feller. This is no time to pitch a hissy." The horse had a hump in its back, but made no offer to buck as Will turned it toward the herd. "Behave your fool self now."

Lightning flashed again, accompanied by a low rumble from the west. The cattle were nothing more than dark blobs in the night, and there wasn't another rider in sight. Will called softly, "Hey, Clint, you here somewhere?"

"I'm here, Will. Over here. Better give 'em plenty of room tonight. Some of these lead steers are feelin' sassy. Won't take much to start 'em runnin'."

"I'm ridin' my best horse, old Scrappy. He's an ornery sonofabitch, but he likes to run."

"Ever been in a stampede, Will?"

"Yeah, once."

"Lots of fun, ain't it?"

"Not one damn little bit."

The two men were about fifty feet apart as they talked in low tones. Clint said, "They always run in the dark. I've been in a couple of stampedes and both of 'em was in the damned dark."

Trying to joke, Will said, "I don't know if cattle are afraid of the dark, but it scares the hell out of me." He realized it wasn't much of a joke.

The two men went their separate ways. Will whistled something tuneless to let other night guards know where he was. Another flash of lightning lit up the western sky. A few seconds later thunder boomed.

"Christ on a stick," someone said.

They were soon joined by the rest of the crew. Lucas Porter had seen the danger and had everybody mounted. "If they run," he yelled, "try to keep 'em goin' north."

A brilliant flash of lightning showed most of the cattle were on their feet. Thunder boomed like cannon fire.

"They're gonna run," a man yelled.

It was as if the thunder was a starting gun. Two thousand eight hundred cattle were instantly running. Wild. Crazy. Men yelled, but their voices were drowned out in the noise of pounding hooves.

A huge mass of animal bodies surrounded Will. Scrappy sensed the excitement and broke into a full gallop with no urging from his rider. The only times Will could see the other men were when lightning lit up the sky. Everything was a dark blob, a loud rumble.

Long horns clacked as cattle ran into each other in the dark. He reined the bay horse east, hoping to get on one side of the herd, and when he believed he was, he turned the horse north, hoping to catch the leaders.

Scrappy was running his best, hooves pounding, jumping gulleys. Will couldn't see the ground, and was silently thankful for the good night vision the Almighty had given horses. "Watch where you're goin', feller," he said aloud, "but keep goin'."

There was no stopping the cattle. All the cowboys could hope to do was to keep them from scattering. A black sea of cattle was crowding Will now, bearing east. A steer bumped his horse, and the horse staggered but kept its feet. The man and horse had to give ground or the cattle would have knocked them down. The horse would have been gored.

Another flash of lightning showed he was on the east side of the herd, but the herd was crowding him, paying no attention to his yelling. The cattle were scattering.

A pistol shot came from somewhere ahead, and Will pulled hs Russian .44, cocked the hammer back, and fired into the ground near a dark blob. The bay horse didn't like the gunshot near its head. It bounced on its front feet, bucked one jump, then leveled off and continued running. Will fired again, right into the face of a big steer. It was hopeless.

He could hear gunshots and see flashes of gunfire off to his left, away off, and the next zigzag of lightning revealed twenty-eight hundred cattle scattered as far as he could see, running wild.

"How far," Will muttered aloud, "are you brutes gonna run? How far can you run?"

They ran. The bay horse was tiring. The cattle had to be tiring. The horse's front feet dropped into a shallow ravine and it almost fell. Will felt like swearing, but this was no time to use God's name in vain. The horse kept its balance, climbed out of the ravine, and went on. Lightning lit up the sky and thunder cracked. When it was dark, it was pitch dark. Only the sounds of running hooves and horns knocking together told Will he was somewhere with a bunch of cattle. He didn't know how many cattle and he didn't know where.

And then, finally, when the bay horse had run about as far as it could run, a streak of lightning showed him he and the horse were alone. The cattle were either behind him or to his right. Lifting the reins, he brought the horse to a stop and listened. All he could hear was the horse's hard breathing. A gunshot came from away off to his left, so far away that he could barely hear it. He heard no running cattle.

"Where in this big black world are we, feller?"

The horse stood spraddle legged, its side heaving, as Will dismounted and loosened the cinches. "No use tryin' to find anything in the dark," Will said to the horse. "A man couldn't find his ass with both hands. We'll have to wait for daylight, and right here is as good a place to wait as any. Wonder if there's anybody else around."

To find out, he pointed the .44 at the sky and pulled the trigger. The shot boomed. He listened. No answer.

"You don't reckon we're all that's left alive, do you feller? Get your wind and rest easy. It's a long time till daylight."

Chapter Twelve

Sitting on the ground among the sagebrush and the yucca, Will waited. It occurred to him that if a grass fire was started on this side of the river, they'd lose some cattle. Maybe a lot of cattle. The bay horse stood with its head down, sides still heaving, nostrils flared.

But the danger of a fire soon ended. Instead, it rained.

He could hear it coming. The lightning and thunder were simultaneous now. Close. Jagged lightning was hitting the ground, but the rain was drowning out any fires it started. Closer.

The horse was probably the biggest object around and a good target for lightning. Will could do nothing about that. He'd once heard a story about a cowboy whose feet were badly burned when his spurs attracted lightning. He unbuckled his spurs.

The rain came closer, sounding like a hundred drum rolls. Suddenly, Will felt as if a barrel of water had been dumped on him. Solid sheets of rain. Within two seconds he was sopping wet. The horse didn't like the sound or the feel of the rain and danced around at the end of the bridle reins. Then it accepted the rain and stood, head down, a hump in its back.

The rain beat down, drummed the ground, and drowned out the sound of thunder. The only part of

Will that was dry was his head and face under the wide-brimmed hat. Even his socks were soaked.

He sat on the ground until a puddle formed under him. He stood, keeping as far away from the horse as he could and still hang onto the reins. All he could do was wait it out with his shoulders hunched up to his ears. Rain was falling faster than the ground could soak it up, and soon he was standing in water.

Lightning cracked. All he could see was rain. It was like a heavy curtain around him. He wondered how the other men were doing. He wondered how far the cattle had scattered. He wondered how long the rain would last. He hugged himself and waited.

Then, as quickly as it had started, it was over. The lightning and thunder led it east. He could still hear it, moving on. The drum rolls were farther away.

"Boy," he said aloud. "We've been wantin' rain, but not that kind." The kind of short, heavy rain they'd just had would hit the ground and run off into the low places instead of soaking the ground. But it would do some good. It would provide some moisture for the starving grass. And when he looked to the west and saw stars in the sky, Will grinned. "We're still alive, feller. Maybe it was worth it."

At daylight, he tightened the cinches and buckled on his spurs. His boots squished when he moved on the ground, and he was glad to get on the horse. The horse was rested now and eager to be moving. There wasn't a steer or heifer in sight. Nothing but the rolling hills and the yucca. Which way to go?

He believed the main body of the herd was west, but he believed too that some cattle, probably a lot of cattle, had split off and were somewhere east. The cowboys he'd seen in the lightning flashes and the gunfire he'd heard were all to the west. The cattle in that direction would be found. He reined east.

The sun popped up on the eastern horizon and hit him full in the face. It was warm and good. He rode at a trot for a mile and saw a small herd of antelope, but no cattle. A couple more miles, and he topped a low hill, stopped, and studied the terrain. Another long, low hill to the north pointed like a finger at a flat plain where the ground was so level a rabbit couldn't hide. Still no cattle. The rain would have wiped out any tracks the cattle had left, and they were probably busy cropping the grass now and wouldn't make fresh tracks. He reined his horse north.

At the top of the pointing finger he reined up again— and saw them. About two hundred head, a half mile north, grazing peacefully. Dismounting, he stood at rein's distance from the horse, drew his pistol, and fired a shot in the air. No answer.

Mounted again, he said to the horse, "That's a lot of cattle for you and me to move by ourselves, feller, but we can do it."

The bay horse worked hard, constantly loping from one side of the bunch to the other, getting them together, getting them moving west. Will was grateful that the cattle were half-wild and trotted away from him. That many tame cattle would have been impossible for one horseman to handle.

The warm sun had him dry now. Even his feet were dry. The horse was wet, though, wet with sweat. Yelling, whistling, whipping at cattle with his catch rope, Will kept them traveling. At the same time, Will watched the western horizon, hoping to see some cowboys coming to help.

At noon he was tired and hungry, but instead of feeling sorry for himself, he was sorry for the horse. It had been on a run almost constantly for hours, and was tiring fast. "We'll get back to the wagon, feller," Will said, "and when we do you'll get a long rest. That's a promise."

No need to dismount now to fire a shot in the air. The horse was too tired to care. Will fired a shot, noticed he had only one live round in the cylinder, and fired again.

What? What was that? An answer? It came from far away but it was a gunshot. Then another. "They know where we are, feller. They'll be comin' to help."

A half hour later two cowboys rode out of a deep draw, stopped, saw Will, and came toward him at a gallop. Will grinned, "You gents out for a ride?"

"Yeah, it's a nice day for a canter in the park," Clint Overhart said. "We thought we'd take our daily constitutional."

"Where's the outfit?"

"Almost due west. The boss reckoned you'd be over this way and might need some help."

"Did we lose anybody? Or any stock?"

"Don't think so. You're the only one didn't show up for breakfast this mornin'."

"Hell of a rain."

"A turd floater."

She didn't tell her family about fighting off Indians somewhere between the Cimarron River and Dodge City. If she had, they would be horrified and forbid her to go back. Of course, she'd go back anyway, but why have a family fight? She didn't tell them about Will Porter either. Her mother would have worried that she would marry some Texas cowboy, and, God help her, go off to some terrible place like Texas.

She did ask her father and two brothers again and again what Grandfather Mays had told them. She insisted that they repeat every word to the best of their recollection and that they stretch their recollection further.

They had nothing to add.

She went through her grandfather's belongings— what hadn't been disposed of—stored in a big overland trunk in the basement. Not one thing was in it that she hadn't already seen.

She'd go back to Dodge City and take another trip

out onto the prairie. Who knows, she might get lucky. First, though, she had to go see that railroad superintendent. And, oh yes, she wanted to contact some cattle buyers.

Mr. Littleton was out of town, she was told. He was in Wichita, taking care of some business. Where in Wichita? He was staying in the Great Western Hotel, and would be there for several days.

All right, she'd stop in Wichita. Will had said they originally planned to go to Wichita. Cattle buyers were plentiful there. But where in Wichita did one find cattle buyers? At the packing houses? Come to think of it, she didn't know what kind of cattle Will and his crew were bringing up from Texas. Were they beeves for slaughter, or cows and calves, or what? Gosh damn, how stupid can a body get? She should have asked. Now, if she found some cattle buyers, she was not only going to look stupid, she was going to feel stupid. They wouldn't take her seriously. They'd laugh at her.

All right, let them laugh. All she wanted to know was whom Will and his uncle could wire from Dodge City.

It was an all-night ride to Wichita in the swaying, rattling passenger coach, but that was better than riding a long night and most of the next day to Dodge City. In fact, breaking the trip to Dodge into two separate trips would make it easier. At Wichita, she took a room at the Great Western Hotel, asked a clerk in a striped shirt if Mr. Littleton was in his room, and was told that he was not. Next she inquired where the cattle yards were, then took a hansom there.

The cattle pens covered almost ten acres, and a cloud of dust hung over the whole place. At the Livestock Exchange Building, she walked down a hall until she came to a door with a sign painted on it that read Goodwin & Sons Livestock Co. She opened the door and stepped inside.

Four heads were bent over desks when she entered, and immediately they looked up, puzzled. They were

98

all men. "Excuse me," she said, "I'm looking for a cattle buyer?"

They only stared.

"Excuse me," she said louder. "Is there a cattle buyer here?"

Finally a middle-aged man with a bald head and a mustache said, "He's out in the yards, Miss."

"Would you please tell me where in the yards, and what his name is?"

"They're unloading some cattle over there." He pointed east. "His name is Mr. Goodwin."

She forced herself to smile sweetly. "Thank you very much."

From the steps of the Exchange Building, she could see railcars spotted between some pens, and she could see and hear men yelling at cattle. To get there, she had to walk down a dusty alley beween two rows of pens, and her patent leather slippers and the hem of her dress were soon covered with dust. And it wasn't just dust. There were cattle droppings. Cow pies. Some fresh. "Oh-o-o," she moaned.

The first man she came to saw her coming and stared with his mouth open. "Sir, can you tell me where I might find Mr. Goodwin?" Without speaking, he pointed at a stout man in a business suit. "Thank you very much." She want on, wishing to God she'd worn her lace-up, high-top shoes, wishing she could dress like a man.

"Mr. Goodwin?" He wore a finger-length gray coat and a vest with a gold watch chain draped from one side to the other. He was looking between some corral poles at a pen full of cattle.

"Huh?" Sweat was running from under his homburg hat down his red beefy face.

"Sir, are you Mr. Goodwin?"

"That I am, miss. Who might you be?"

"I am Lucina Mays. I am looking for a cattle buyer."

"You've got some cattle to sell?"

"Well, no sir, I haven't, but an acquaintance is driving twenty-eight hundred head to Dodge City from West Texas."

"To Dodge City?" He stared at her in disbelief.

She wanted to tell him to, for God's sake, quit staring. Instead, she said, "Yes. They will arrive in a few days."

"Twenty-eight hundred head? From West Texas?"

Patiently, she said, "Yes sir."

"Nobody's shipping cattle from Dodge City."

"They will be. As a matter of fact, sir, Dodge City will soon become the new Abilene."

"Is that a fact?" He took a large blue handkerchief out of a hip pocket and mopped his face.

"Yes sir."

He stared at her for another second, then looked down at the dust and manure. She pressed him. "You can see, sir, that the railroad and the quarantine line are moving west. Dodge City will soon become the cattle-shipping capital of the country."

"Is that a fact?" He was thinking, she could tell. She remained quiet, allowing him to think it over. Finally, he said, "Well, I can't buy cattle unseen. And I ain't making a trip to Dodge City without knowing for certain there are a lot of cattle there to be bought."

"I wouldn't ask you to do that, sir. All I want now is some assurance that you are buying cattle and that you will be willing to travel to Dodge City when the cattle arrive."

"Yes, miss, I am in the business of buying cattle."

"Do you buy all kinds? I mean, do you buy only beeves for slaughter, or do you buy, uh, others?" She wished she hadn't asked that question. Her ignorance showed. Then she was glad she did.

"I buy all kinds, miss. I buy slaughter cattle and I buy young stuff that I can resell to the farmers."

"The farmers?"

"Yes, ma'am." Now he was talking like a father to a

100

daughter. "These farmers grow more corn than they know what to do with, and they can make a profit buying Texas cattle, feeding them through the winter, and selling them in the spring."

"Oh?" Now she was staring. "Oh, uh, sir, would you please tell me your full name and where you can be reached by wire?" She opened her pocketbook and took out her pencil and notepad. He told her. She wrote it down.

But as she made her way back to the Great Western Hotel, her shoes filthy, her dress full of dust, her face streaked with dirt, it occurred to her that she had accomplished nothing. Will and his uncle wouldn't want to do business by wire. They'd travel to Wichita or Kansas City themselves and find their own buyer.

Lucina Mays, she told herself, you are sticking your nose into something that is none of your business. You are working yourself into a lather for nothing.

Chapter Thirteen

Now that they were north of the Cimarron, Will pointed the herd in a westerly direction. His uncle Lucas agreed that it would be better to hold the cattle on the prairie west of Dodge City while shipping arrangements were made. The rain had started the buffalo grass growing again, and the whole country was green and pretty. Good country. Good grass. The kind of grass that, given enough moisture, held its nutrition the year around. And over west there was no question that the land was public domain and belonged to whoever homesteaded it or grazed livestock on it.

They crossed a creek that had been nearly dry when Will crossed it before and was now a narrow but flowing stream. The cattle watered, grazed, and bedded down peacefully. The remuda was feeling better too now that the grass was green. The cowboys were looking in the direction of Dodge City as if they hoped to see someone coming. Anyone.

"We're almost there, ain't we, Will?" asked the cowboy named Clint Overhart. "Reckon old Lucas'll let us go to town and hoist a few?"

"Don't know why not. It doesn't take a dozen men to hold a herd of cattle in this country."

"Feller's got to go to town once in a while and wet his swaller pipe and warsh his socks."

Knowing what he meant, Will had to grin. "There's plenty of washerwomen around, servicin' the buffalo hunters. They oughtta be glad to service a man who doesn't smell like a packin' house."

The two men were saddling their horses, preparing to take the early night guard. They were about the same size and were dressed the same, only Clint was older, and he carried a short-barreled Colt .44 in a well-worn holster low on his hip. His horse lunged backward when he pulled the cinch tight. "Sonofabitch," Clint swore. "Whoa now."

"He's a little cinchy," Will allowed.

Clint knew Lucas Porter wouldn't stand for anyone abusing the horses, and he took the blame. "My own fault. I know he's cinchy, but I had my mind on town. Whoa now." He stood close to the horse and pulled straight up on the latigo, pulled it slow and steady. The horse, a short-backed bay, swelled up but didn't move out of its tracks. "The town's full of buffalo hunters, you say?"

"It was. I ain't seen a buffalo lately, and they might have moved on south by now. If they have, the hunters've moved with 'em and the whores are gonna be glad to see you comin'."

"Wal, I'll git a bath in hot water and a haircut and some clean clothes and sprinkle some of that toilet water on myself and maybe I won't scare 'em out of the country."

They mounted and rode at a trot toward the herd about two hundred yards away. "Don't forget," Will said, "there's a marshal in Dodge City who hates cowboys."

"You mentioned him before. A town marshal, huh?"

"Yeah. He said he was a deputy marshal in Abilene and now he's the marshal in Dodge City, and he ain't gonna let no Texas cowboys tear up his town."

"I been up to Abilene a couple times, and there was some shootin', all right, but I ain't so sure the cowboys

103

started it. Some of these lawdogs're so full of the law and stuff they think they're God almighty."

"He looks like a tough little sonofabitch."

"Some of 'em once had the notion they was gonna take the guns away from ever'body that rode a hoss down the street. Ha. They wanted us to shuck our guns while ever' card slick, barkeep, footpad, and cheap crook had guns right where they could reach 'em. We was s'posed to be sittin' ducks."

"What happened?"

"There was some powder burnt, three men kilt, one of 'em a deputy sheriff, but we kept our irons."

They rode silently a moment, and before they went their separate ways, Will on one side of the herd and Clint on the other, Clint asked, "What's this gent's name?"

"Damned if I know. He introduced himself to me, but we didn't trade names. Matter of fact, he was downright unsociable."

This was embarrassing, and getting worse by the minute. Lucina Mays had sent the hotel clerk upstairs to ask Mr. Hiram Littleton to meet her in the lobby. That was after she'd scrubbed her shoes until most of the color came off and some of the dirt and manure. She'd changed into the one clean dress she had with her. Now, as she sat in a padded chair and Hiram Littleton sat in another, he was asking questions she couldn't answer.

She had no idea. How many cattle could one get into a railcar? She felt herself slumping in her chair, and forced herself to sit up straight. "Well, uh, Mr. Littleton, judging from your years of experience, how many cattle do you believe will fit comfortably?" She knew she didn't say that right.

"Fit comfortably? Well now, that depends on the size

104

of the cattle and their hornspan. What are you talking about, Miss Mays, grown stuff or dogies?"

"Dogies? Uh, I don't think . . ."

"You haven't seen the cattle?"

"Oh no," she answered quickly, "I have no financial interest in them at all."

"I see. Hmm. Well at any rate, I have been able to locate only about forty cattle cars that I can send to Dodge City in the near future. More will be available later. Will that do?"

"I, uh, I'm sure that will be, uh, better than nothing. Are you certain that more will be available in the not-too-distant future?"

"Yes, Miss Mays. I am sure that we can find enough cars eventually."

"Fine." She had to sit up straight again. "Now, about shipping pens?"

"I'll have a crew there within a week or ten days building some pens."

"Well, that's fine, Mr. Littleton." Lucina stood and offered her hand. "We'll be looking for the cars and the building crew."

He took her hand gently. "Will your grandfather, Mr. Rathman, be with you?"

"No sir, I am leaving for Dodge City in the morning, and I will meet with my cattleman friend there."

"Oh." the railroad superintendent was disappointed. "Give my regards to Mr. Rathman."

"Indeed I will, sir."

As she slipped into her nightdress and turned down the bedcovers, she knew she had sounded ignorant and unsure of herself, not the way a well-informed businesswoman was supposed to sound. But she had accomplished something. Twice now, Mr. Littleton had promised cattle cars and shipping pens. He

105

couldn't renege now.

If he did, so help her God, she'd take her rifle and shoot him.

It was late afternoon when they reached the mighty Arkansas. Lucas Porter reckoned it had rained up in those Colorado mountains where the river was born and the water was running downhill all the way to Kansas and beyond. He wanted to get the cattle across before dark, and the cowboys started to strip and loosen saddle cinches.

"Rider's comin'," a cowboy said.

All hands stopped what they were doing and watched the rider come from the direction of Dodge City. When he got closer they could see the silver star on his vest.

"Evenin'," Lucas Porter said.

The rider reined up and sat his saddle still, a scowl on his face. "You plannin' to cross this river with them cattle?"

"Yes sir, that's what we're fixin' to do."

"Well, you can't."

Will Porter was stripped down to his shorts, which made him feel helpless, but he rode over to see what was happening. The marshal turned unfriendly eyes to him. "I told you we ain't allowin' no Texas cattle around here."

"I heard you."

"Well, you ain't crossin' this river with 'em."

Lucas Porter said, "Will, is this the town marshal you told us about?"

"Yeah."

Looking beyond the marshal, the older Porter said, "That's free range over there, ain't it?"

"It's claimed."

"By who?"

"It's been homesteaded."

"I don't see no houses or nothin'. Nobody's done anything to prove up on a homestead." Turning back to Will, Lucas Porter said, "Whatta you think, Will?"

Knowing he was vulnerable without his clothes and gun, Will gazed across the river, at the marshal, at his uncle. He was terribly uncomfortable, and he wished his uncle hadn't put him in this position. But as it was he had to say something. Speaking with a drawl, he said, "It doesn't look swimmin' deep, but it won't be easy to cross. What I'm thinkin' is the railroad's on the other side, and we'll probably have to ship cattle a few hundred at a time. I don't care to cross the river that many times."

"Exactly what I'm thinkin'," his uncle said. "Now marshal or whatever you are, I think you're out of your jurisdiction. But if you can show me that that country over there has been legally claimed, we'll stay over here. Otherwise we're goin' across."

With menace in his voice, the marshal said, "You'll be sorry."

"Whatta you mean by that?" Lucas Porter was scowling now.

"You'll see." The marshal turned his horse around and went on a lope back toward Dodge City.

"All right, boys," Lucas Porter yelled, "let's get 'em in the water before that gentleman comes back with an army."

Will was on his best swimming horse, a gray gelding named Ghost because of the way he looked in the dark. But the water didn't come any higher than Will's knees when he was in the saddle. He and Ghost waded the river with the leaders, then turned around and waded back to help get the rest of the cattle in the water. On the third trip, Ghost tipped onto his side and Will swallowed a mouthful of the muddy Arkansas. Sputtering and coughing, he grabbed hold of Ghost's tail and let the horse pull him across. He had to gag and cough a while before he could get back on the horse, but he had to cross the river again.

Finally, just before darkness settled over the wide Kansas prairie, all the cattle were safely on the north side of the river. Then came the wagon. With a team of big horses pulling and cowboys' ropes dallied around saddle horns, the wagon was floated and pulled across.

Wet men wanted to gather around the cooking fire, but they knew better than to get in China Eye's way, and they stayed on one side of it.

The talk that evening was about town, and the men wanted to know when they could ride into Dodge City and enjoy the fruits of their labor.

"Well, boys," Lucas Porter began, "we're at the end of a long cattle drive and it has been hard, but we're mightly lucky that we haven't lost a man. Now, I know you've earned the right to go to town, and I intend for you to go, but I'd appreciate it if you'd stay with the herd for a couple of days until Will can go to town and see if we can get the railcars and pens. Will has advised me that we might have to wait a few days. If we do, you can go to town a few at a time while we wait. How's that?"

"That's fine with me," China Eye allowed. "I've been up the trail before, and I ain't in no hurry to give my wages to them card slicks and justices of the peace."

"Yeah, I heard about that," a cowboy said. "I ain't givin' up my wages."

"They'll skin you, boys," China Eye went on, his one good eye going from man to man. "If you got anything left after the faro dealers git through with you, some lawdog'll arrest you for stubbin' your toe on the sidewalk, and some justice of the peace'll fine you whatever you've got left."

"That's the truth, fellers," Clint Overhart put in. "There's a lot of folks in these trail towns that live high on what they can skin the cowboys out of."

"I'm a-gittin' too old to go up the trail again," added China Eye, "and I'm figgurin' on goin' back to Texas with my wages in my pocket."

"Will's going to leave first thing in the morning," Lucas Porter said. "We ought to know by tomorrow night what the deal is about them cattle cars."

"Hoist one for me, Will," a cowboy said. "Make it a straight shot, no water, no beer, just whiskey."

"Take mine with a swaller of beer, then warsh it down with a shot of whiskey," said another.

"And if you see one of them faro slicks, tell 'im his brethren owes me some chips and I'm a-comin' to collect."

Will chuckled. "If I do all that, I might not get back."

Dodge City was quiet when Will rode down Trail Street at midmorning. Two freight wagons passed each other, and both were empty. Two men on horseback came from the east end of the street and stopped when they saw Will. One was the bulldog he'd almost tangled with in the Longbranch. He didn't recognize the other, who wore baggy wool pants, a wool shirt, a dirty white hat, and flat-heeled jackboots. Both had six-guns on their hips and Winchester rifles in saddle boots. A long bullwhip was coiled and tied to Bulldog's saddle. They gave Will hard looks as he rode by, but said nothing.

After riding the length of Trail Street, along the railroad, Will feared the worst. There were no cattle cars. Just to be sure, he went to the depot and asked the station agent. No, he was told, not cattle cars and nobody building pens.

Next, he went in search of Lucina Mays. She'd been on his mind every day, and he wanted to see her again anyway. He hoped she'd have an explanation. At the Dodge House he tied his horse to a hitchrail, stepped up onto the long porch, and went inside. No, Miss Mays had left eight days earlier and had not returned.

"Of all the fools who ever lived, I lead the goddam parade," Will muttered under his breath as he went back out to the horse. I would have sworn she really meant what she said. Why in hell was I damfool enough to believe some girl? What am I gonna tell Lucas?

He started to untie his horse, then changed his mind and walked back to the depot, spurs ringing. There he sent a telegraph to Mr. Hiram Littleton at Kansas City. There was nothing to do then but wait for an answer. He hated waiting.

The saloons looked inviting. A man could kill some time in a saloon. No, he might run into the bulldog and his sidekick. This was no time for a brawl. Well, there were the washerwomen. That was the only sex he was going to get a chance at for no telling how long. But a mental picture of Lucina Mays came to his mind, and the washerwomen were repulsive by comparison.

Aw hell, she'd gone back to Kansas City and he wouldn't see her again anyway. She'd thought she had some cattle cars arranged and when she found out she didn't, she'd skinned out of there, not wanting to have to apologize. Might as well forget her, Will Porter. Try to, anyway.

Still, he couldn't get her out of his mind, and those whores just wouldn't do. They wouldn't do at all.

An idea came to him. Go to the livery barn and see if her horses were there. If she'd skinned out for good, she'd have sold her horses first. Old Easton at the livery barn ought to know.

They recognized each other immediately. "Say, young feller," the short man said, pushing his hat back and wiping sweat off his forehead with a shirtsleeve. "You was right about that fight at Adobe Walls. I went on down there and shore enough, there'd been a hell of a shootout. They had thirteen Indian heads to show for it."

"That battle will be talked about for a lot of years to come," Will allowed as he dismounted in front of the barn.

"They said you was there and done your share of the fightin'."

"Yeah."

"There was some boys come up from the south somewheres and they said they didn't see nothin' of old Quanah. Ever'body figgers he's scared of Colonel Miles and his soldier boys and he's hidin' out, either in the Indian Nation or way out on those Staked Plains in Texas."

"I hope he stays there. Say, I, uh, was wonderin' about Miss Mays. You know, the young lady that kept two horses here? Are they still here?"

"Yep. In that pen yonder."

"She didn't sell 'em or anything?"

"Nope. Far as I know she still owns 'em, but I ain't seen her for a spell."

"You reckon she's quit the country?"

The livery owner studied the ground a moment. "Wish I knowed." He looked up. "She's a purty one, ain't she?"

"Yeah," Will grinned, "when she doesn't try to look like a man." But while he was grinning, bitter thoughts were going through his mind. She had left her horses here but she was gone.

The short livery-owner frowned thoughtfully for a moment. "Reckon why she does that? Try to look like a man."

"It's a puzzler to me."

"She's a purty one, but she's a quare one."

Glad to have someone to talk to while he was waiting for an answer to his telegraph, Will told the short man about the herd of Texas longhorns out west of town a half dozen or so miles, and asked about a tough-looking farmer who had a herd of Durham cattle somewherer north of town. What he learned was interesting.

"He ain't no farmer. He's a hired man. Him and eight or ten hard cases came out here from somewhere back east and homesteaded several sections. They built some sod shacks and some pens and next thing we knew they had a couple hundred head of them red cattle up there."

111

"A hired man?"

"Yeah. Word is them gents was paid by some eastern moneybags."

"That's legal, ain't it? The land's open for homesteadin'?"

"Far as we know."

"Where up north is their land?"

"Along Walnut Creek. Good country."

"And folks think they're bein' bankrolled by some easterner?"

"Have to be. They come to town ever' few days. Them gents ain't hardscrabble farmers."

"Well, I'll be damned."

By evening, Will knew he was not going to get an answer to his wire that day, and he left the depot to get on his horse and go back to the wagon. He was trying to think of a way to break the news to his uncle when he noticed the horse was gone.

He'd left it at a hitchrail in front of the Dodge House and it wasn't there.

"Hawy, haw. What good's a cowpuncher without a horse? Haw, haw." They'd come up behind him and were sitting on their horses, the bulldog and his sidekick.

Will faced them. "Did you do somethin' to my horse?"

"Do somethin' to 'im? Haw, haw. Last time I seen 'im he was haulin' ass down the street."

"He shore can jump," the sidekick said.

Hands on hips, looking the the bulldog in the eye, Will demanded, "What did you do to him?" Before they could answer, he knew. The bullwhip that had been tied to the fork of Bulldog's saddle was now hanging, coiled, around the saddle horn.

"Did you whip that horse?"

"Haw, haw. What're you gonna do about it?"

Here it was, an ultimatum. Fight or turn tail. Will glanced down the street and saw his horse a block

112

away. It had stepped on a bridle rein and stopped. He also saw the marshal off to his right, just standing there with an amused expression on his face. Other men were standing on the plank walk, curious. It was a fight Will couldn't win. It was a fight he couldn't avoid.

Hissing through his teeth, he said, "Get down."

"Haw, haw. What're you gonna do, shoot me with that purty white pistol?"

"I don't need a gun to whip your ass."

"Haw, haw." And suddenly, Bulldog had a six-gun in his hand. He had drawn his gun so fast that Will didn't even get a hand on his. "Haw, haw. You're gonnna do what?"

The man was a gunfighter. Will had no chance at all. His mind racing, he tried to decide what to do. Try to draw the Russian .44 out of its high holster? Suicide. Try to talk the man into a fistfight? He'd tried that. Finally, he said, lips stiff:

"I'll tell you what you can do, you can go take a flyin' hump at a rollin' wagon wheel." With that, he turned on his heels and walked toward his horse, half expecting a bullet in the back.

When he got to the horse he gathered the reins and stepped into the saddle. Looking back, he saw that no one had moved. They were watching him.

"You sons of bitches got by with it this time," he muttered under his breath. "But there'll be another meeting."

Chapter Fourteen

Will Porter and his uncle Lucas decided after a breakfast of hotcakes, bacon, and coffee that one of them would have to take the train to Kansas City and try to arrange for some cattle cars. Will was not proud of his performance so far and he admitted it to his uncle. But Lucas Porter insisted that he go.

"You're gonna have to learn to do some sellin'," the older Porter said. "Raisin' beef is only part of the job of makin' a livin'. You have to sell 'em too."

"Yeah, but . . ."

"You do your best."

He dreaded it. It wasn't the long train ride. He might enjoy watching the country roll by while he sat in a passenger car. What worried him was meeting with a big augur in a city office and trying to sell him on the idea of sending cattle cars to Dodge City. If he had to talk for a living he'd starve. Then he remembered the sales talk Lucina Mays said she had thrown at the railroad superintendent. That sounded good. Maybe, coming from a man who could promise the cattle, it would work. If he could talk straight.

Still, it was worrisome. It was downright scary. His uncle depended on him, and if he failed again, he'd have a hard time living with himself.

The eastbound, he knew, pulled out late in the

evening. It rolled all night and all the next day. He'd leave his horse at the livery barn, and wear his cleanest clothes. Aw hell. He had no clean clothes. He was not only going to look and talk like a country hick, he was going to smell like one.

For a few seconds he resented his uncle sending him to Kansas City. But only for a few seconds. The older Porter was right. If he was going to be in the cattle business he had to learn to take care of business.

The herd was scattered over several square miles and grazing peacefully. Lucas Porter and some of the crew were gathered around the wagon when Will saddled up and prepared to begin his journey.

"Somebody's comin'," a cowboy said, and all eyes turned to the east.

It was a man on a horse. Or a boy. He was so far away that the cowboys couldn't tell.

"Looks like a kid," someone said as the figure drew closer.

"It is a kid. What's a kid doin' around here?"

"Holy jumpin' rattlesnakes," Will exclaimed. "It's her."

Everyone stopped what he was doing and stared open-mouthed as Lucina Mays rode up. She was wearing her baggy boy's clothes and a big hat. Finally, Will came out of his trance and went over to her.

"Howdy, Miss Mays. What brings you out to the cattle country?" He offered to help her off her horse, but she dismounted without his help.

"I just got back to Dodge City last night. The train was late. And I heard you were looking for me. Mr. Easton at the livery barn said you were out here and he guessed you were along the river."

"Yes, uh . . ." Will turned to the cowboys. "Ain't you yahoos got anything to do but stare at a lady?" Embarrassed, the crew suddenly got busy doing other things, anything. Will apologized. "They haven't seen a lady for a long time."

"It's all right, I'm getting used to it."

Lucas Porter walked over, spurs ringing.

Instead of waiting for him to introduce himself, Lucina Mays held out her right hand. "You would be Mr. Porter. I am Lucina Mays. Will has told me about you."

Surprised at her boldness, the older Porter hesitated a second before taking her hand. He shook it once. "Pleased to, uh, meet you, Miss Mays. Will told me about you too. I, uh . . ."

The cowboys couldn't help stealing a glance now and then.

Again she surprised them and didn't wait for their anticipated question. "The cattle cars have been promised. Also a crew to build stock pens. I expect them any day now."

"Well, that's fine, Miss Mays, uh . . ." Lucas Porter was still flustered.

Will said, "I sent a wire to Hiram Littleton in Kansas City. I didn't get an answer. Not yet, anyhow."

"You won't. He's in Wichita for the time being. I met with him there just a few days ago and he repeated his commitment."

"Then," said Lucas Proter, "it's all settled?"

"Yes sir, Mr. Porter. I'm sure Mr. Littleton won't renege. However, it may be a few days before anything happens."

"We don't mind waitin' a few days." The older Porter nodded toward a small bunch of grazing cattle. "These brutes are puttin' on some beef here."

"Well, I must get back." She turned toward her horse.

"Won't you have a cup of coffee, Miss Mays?" Lucas Porter asked. "Old China Eye will be pleased to pour you a cup. We're gonna have some supper here about sundown, and you're more than welcome to stay."

"I appreciate your offer, Mr. Porter, but I must get back before dark. I'm happy your cattle are here."

116

"Would you like somebody to ride back with you?"

"Oh no. I can manage, thank you." With that, she mounted the horse. "Will you be coming into town soon?"

"Yes, ma'am. One of us will be in tomorrow."

"Please come to see me." She rode away.

Everyone was staring again. Then Will said, "Ever see anybody like her before?"

"No," Lucas Porter drawled, "I can't say I have."

"Whatta you think of her?"

"Wal, I've always been leery of women that try to take the place of a man. But . . ." He didn't finish, only shrugged and shook his head.

"She's a woman, all right. You ought to see her in a dress."

Lucas Porter continued shaking his head, a half grin on his face.

Will said, "Ain't she somethin'?"

The next time he saw her she was wearing a dress. He waited until evening to ride into Dodge City, figuring there couldn't be anything new until the westbound arrived. He intended to go to the Dodge House and see Lucina Mays, but not until after he saw what the train had brought.

It was there. The engine was standing just west of the depot, hissing and steaming. To the horse Will was riding, the engine looked like a horrifying beast, and it danced nervously. "It's harmless, feller," Will said to the animal, but he rode on the opposite side of Trail Street, as far from the engine as he could get. On down the track a ways, toward the end of a string of railcars, he saw a flatcar loaded with building materials—creosoted fence posts and two-inch lumber. That, he hoped, was the material for building stock pens. There were no cattle cars, however. Oh well, no need for cattle cars until a pen and loading chute were built.

He didn't have to look for Lucina Mays as he rode back up the street. She saw him. "Yoohoo," she shouted from the porch of the Dodge House. "Oh, Will." She was wearing the long blue dress again. Damn she was pretty.

With a broad grin on his face, Will reined over, tied up, and walked up onto the porch. "If what I see down there is what I hope it is, we're in business, Miss Mays."

"Lucina, darn it. Or Lu."

"Whatever you say, Lucina."

"Anything but Lucy. Did you see some cattle cars?"

"No, but there's a car carryin' the kind of lumber that can be used to build a corral."

"I want to see it."

"Well, you'll have to walk a ways, and in that outfit . . . the street is pretty dusty."

"I've walked in the dirt before." She smiled. "You'd be surprised at some of the stuff I've walked in, Will Porter."

They stayed on the planks until they came to the end of the sidewalk, then they walked in the street side by side. Will wished she'd take his arm the way he believed a lady was supposed to, but she didn't. Instead, she held the hem of her dress off the ground with both hands. Her shoes were not the slippers Will had seen before, but were the high-topped buttoned kind.

At the railcar, she asked, "Is that what it takes to build cattle pens?"

"There's everything that's needed. Plenty of posts and planks. All it takes now is manpower."

"I saw who got out of the passenger car, and I didn't see anyone who looked like working men."

"Maybe the railroad'll hire some men from around here." Will chuckled. "I hope old Littleton ain't expectin' our cowboys to build it. A cowboy ain't worth a nickel off his horse."

"No, I don't think so. No, the pens will belong to the railroad and the railroad will have to build them."

"Whew," Will feigned relief. "For a second there I thought I might have to dig some postholes."

Chuckling, she said, "You'll be spared that for the time being." She turned to face him. "What are your plans? After the cattle are shipped, I mean."

"Dunno. I like cattle and horses."

"Do you own a ranch or do you work for your uncle?"

"It's his outfit. All of it. All I own are a couple of horses, a saddle, and a bedroll. And two guns."

"Most of the land around here is open for homesteading, you know."

"Now that's an idea. But," he chuckled, "you can't graze very many cattle on a hundred and sixty acres, and I can't see myself followin' a plow."

"So you'll go back to Texas." It was a statement, not a question.

"I reckon. That's the best I can think of to do."

"Maybe, before you get all those cattle on their way to market, you'll think of something else."

"Maybe, but not likely."

He didn't stay in town that night. He didn't even stay for supper in the Dodge House restaurant. When he got back to the wagon and offsaddled his horse, he told his uncle about the railcar loaded with building materials. It wouldn't be long now, he allowed. Later that night, after China Eye had washed the dishes in a galvanized tub, Lucas Porter named six cowboys who, he said, could catch their best horses in the morning and go see what there was to see in Dodge City. He promised the rest of the crew they could go in a day or two.

A cowboy suggested they cut cards to see who went first, and that touched off a round of joking. "Whose cards," a man asked. "yours?"

"Hell, old Jackson knows where ever' ace is in that deck."

"I'll let old China Eye draw for me. He can feel an ace

119

they way he can feel a growed-over brand."

"How much'll you give me?" China Eye asked.

"Buy you a drink of whiskey."

"No, boys," Lucas Porter put in. "I've named the men that'll go first."

There was no more said about it.

Six men rode east next morning, their pockets full of silver money that Lucas Porter had taken out of an iron box in the wagon. Wanting to keep track of the cattle, Will caught a long-legged sorrel horse and rode west along the river. He rode until he saw no more sign of cattle, then turned north, saw about fifty head, and pushed them east a mile. Then he turned west again. Ahead of him another member of the crew was hazing cattle east, and Will loped over and helped. The Kansas prairie was as flat as West Texas. Tall, yellow sunflowers grew everywhere. By noon he reckoned he had been as far west and north as the cattle grazed, and he headed back to the wagon.

Only four other men were there: Lucas Porter, China Eye, and two cowboys. Then China Eye left, walking rapidly toward the cottonwoods and the tall grass along the river. Other men were herding the remuda two miles west.

"Good grass," Will allowed, as he filled his tin plate from the pots that China Eye had left hanging over a fire.

"Wonder what the winters are like here?" Lucas Porter said.

"Dunno. This far north it could be colder'n a witch's ass."

"Prob'ly is."

"Company's comin'," a cowboy said.

There were eight riders coming from the northeast. Eyes straining, the men around the wagon tried to make out who and what they were. When the riders got

120

closer, the men could see that they all wore long linen coats, the kind that businessmen used to keep their clothes clean when they took a dusty ride.

"Why would anybody be wearin' coats in this heat?" a cowboy asked.

"Damned if I know. Don't make no sense."

"Uh-oh," Will said. "I've seen that ugly one on the brown horse before. He's a troublemaker."

The cowboys watched curiously as the eight riders came up, all abreast. Without a word spoken by either side, they dismounted. Then before the cowboys could blink back their astonishment, the eight whipped back their coats and yanked short double-barreled shotguns from their belts.

The guns had bores that looked to be as big as the ends of tomato cans. Nervous fingers were on the triggers.

Bulldog had his squinty eyes fixed on Will. He said, "I told you we ain't allowin' no goddam Texas cattle around here."

Chapter Fifteen

Will Porter glanced at his uncle. Lucas Porter gave him a barely perceptible nod. Will knew his uncle was leaving it up to him to make the first move. Or speak the first words. He tried to put some resolve in his voice.

"Well, we're here."

"Not for long, you ain't. Not unless you wanta be buried here."

"You think you're gonna run us off?"

"Yeah, you're goddam right. You round up them bony brutes and git across the river or we'll do it for you."

Shaking his head, Will said, "Not just yet. We're gonna move 'em out of here but they're goin' by rail."

Bulldog took a step closer. "Then, by God, you'll die right now."

It couldn't happen, Will thought. Not after everything else, the fight at Adobe Walls and everything. He couldn't be shot down right here. But yes, it could happen. The twin bores of the shotgun looked even bigger. His heart was beating too fast, and his knees were trembling.

He tried to sound brave, but his voice was wavery. "Why don't you and me fight it out? you got guts enough to do that?"

Bulldog's lips skinned back in a cruel grin. "I could whup you with one hand, but we ain't got time. Say your prayers, cowboy."

A shot came from the direction of the river. All heads swiveled in that direction. No one could see exactly where the shot had come from. Then another shot, and a bullet kicked up dust in front of Bulldog's boots. Bulldog jumped back. The shotgun was turned away from Will.

China Eye yelled, "There's a whole crew here behind these trees and we've got you in our gunsights."

"Huh?" Bulldog grunted, "I don't see nobody."

"We're here behind these trees and you're out in the open where we can't miss. Now git."

Shotguns were pointed down now, and the men in long coats were looking nervously toward the river. But Bulldog wasn't through. "They're bluffin'. There ain't but one man over there. Prob'ly went over there to take a shit, and all he's got's a six-shooter."

Lucas Porter spoke, "We're all well armed, and we're ready to fight. We didn't drive these cattle all the way from West Texas to be run off by a bunch of farmers."

"You're bluffin'." But the shotgun didn't look so dangerous now.

"If there's any shootin' you'll get some of us, but you'll all be dead when the dust settles."

Another shot came from the river, and Bulldog turned his double-barreled gun in that direction. Will moved. He took two fast steps right at Bulldog. Got his hands on the shot gun, twisted, brought his right knee up into Bulldog's crotch. Bulldog grunted in pain, held onto the gun.

A blast from the shotgun hit the ground and kicked up a clod of dirt. The second barrel blasted, and again the shot hit the ground.

Six-guns appeared in the hands of the cowboys and hammers were cocked back. Everyone froze. Everyone but Will and Bulldog.

The shot gun was useless now, and Bulldog let go of it and grabbed for his sidearm. Will had the shotgun in both hands and he jerked the stock up fast. It connected with a loud "crack" against the side of the man's head. Bulldog sat down hard.

But he wasn't out, and he clawed for his pistol. He had it in his hand. Another smashing blow from the shotgun stock knocked him back—flat. He lay still.

Will dropped the shotgun, reached down and picked up Bulldog's pistol, straightened up. Glancing around, he saw his uncle and two cowboys with six-guns in their hands and the men in long coats standing motionless with their guns pointed down.

Lucas Porter said, "All right. Now. You men put those scatterguns on the ground, and don't let a one of 'em fire. One shot and somebody dies."

The men in long coats glanced at each other.

"Do it right now, goddam it."

The hammers were still back on the shotguns, but the men placed them carefully on the ground.

"Get back away from 'em." Then, "All right, China Eye, come on out."

China Eye stepped from around a cottonwood and waded through the tall weeds toward them. A man swore, "Goddam, there is only one."

"Yeah," Lucas Porter said, "but there's more of us not far from here, and every man's got a Winchester repeatin' gun. Now, here's what you're gonna do. You're gonna leave those scatterguns right where they are and you're gonna get on your horses and go back to wherever you came from. We know where your outfit is and if any of my men is found shot, we'll come after you. Got that?"

Bulldog groaned and sat up. Blood ran down his face from a cut over his left eye.

"Pick up your partner there and get him on his horse and git," Lucas Porter ordered.

Two pairs of hands helped Bulldog up and half-lifted

him onto his horse. He hung onto the saddle horn with both hands. One of the men got mounted and picked up the reins of Bulldog's horse. The others mounted, turned their horses, and rode away at a walk, going northeast.

When they were a quarter mile away, Lucas Porter allowed, "I was bluffin' when I said we know where their ourfit is. Do you know where it is, Will?"

"No. I heard it's north of Dodge City somewhere. It won't be hard to find."

"Tomorrow I want you to go find it. I wanta know where it is, just in case we have to take the fight to them."

China Eye was reloading his Colt .44. "Them gents is mean sons of bitches. I seen their kind before. They ain't through."

With a sad shake of his head, Lucas Porter said, "I hope we can get these cattle shipped out of here before somebody gets killed."

Nobody slept much that night at the Double O wagon. Six cowboys came back from town after midnight, and two were so drunk they had to have help getting their horses unsaddled. They all had fresh haircuts, which made them look different and made their hats too big. They smelled of bay rum. The sober ones had stories to tell.

"Boy howdy, now that there's a town for workin' men. I mean to tell you, fellers, there's ever' damned thing a man could want."

"Goddam, you boys should a seen me dancin' up a storm with a blond-headed woman. She had jugs on her you could hang your hat on. She smelled like the flowers of spring. I mean, I wanted to put my face between them tits and bawl like a baby."

"I didn't know you could dance like that, Jim. You look like you was choppin' cotton and kickin' t'rantlers off your legs at the same time."

"Hell, another drink of whiskey and I'd of been

125

dancin' and yellin' like a Comanche."

"Old Clint was doin' enough yellin' for all of us till that marshal come along and told 'im to shut his trap."

"Yeah," Clint Overhart said, "that little rooster of a marshal was too handy at orderin' folks around. If you boys hadn't grabbed holt of me I'd give 'im a taste of his own medicine."

"We didn't go to town for fightin' and shootin' and it was time to come back to the wagon anyways."

"Anything new around here?"

The drunken men sobered up immediately when they heard what had happened.

"No? Eight of 'em? Double-barreled scatterguns?"

"Jumpin' Jesus."

"And old China Eye scared 'em off by hisself?"

"Goddam," said Clint Overhart, "I wished I'd a been here."

"Personally," China Eye said, "I'm glad I was where I was. Right behind a cottonwood big enough to stop a cannonball."

At daylight, three cowboys saddled their night horses and went to help bring in the remuda. That done, they were sitting cross-legged on the ground with breakfast plates on their knees when Lucas Porter told them what was on his mind.

"I hate to tell you this, boys, but I think we'd all better stick pretty close. Can't go to town. There's a mean bunch of jaspers over north somewhere and they want us dead. Now that we bested 'em once, they'll be meaner than ever."

"There was eight of 'em? Hell, there's twelve, thirteen of us."

"Yeah, but we ain't always together."

"No, matter where you are, if you hear shootin' come a-runnin'."

"Best thing about this flat land is you can see 'em comin'."

Will Porter scraped his tin plate and dropped it into

China Eye's washtub, then went to the remuda to catch a horse. Clint Overhart followed him. "Want me to go with you, Will?"

"Aw, I don't know. Ask the boss?"

Clint yelled, "Hey boss, think Will might need some company?"

Lucas Porter yelled back, "If you want to, Clint. But don't start nothin'. If you see any of 'em just keep away from 'em."

They rode northeast until they figured they were north of Dodge City, then they turned their horses straight north. The hot Kansas sun beat down, but it was no hotter than West Texas. There were a few low hills in this part of the country and a few creek beds where bushes grew, but a house or a bunch of cattle would be easy to see. The two riders went far around the brush and anyplace else where a man could hide. Two hours' ride north of Dodge City they saw their first red Durham cattle.

"Good gawd," Clint Overhart said, reining up. "Look at them brutes. Ever see so much beef on one cow?"

The cattle were a quarter mile away, but the two cowboys, accustomed to looking across the plains, could see them clearly. Reining up beside Clint, Will squinted through the heat waves. "That's what the beef industry is comin' to, Clint. Some day everbody'll be breedin' that kind of stock."

"They're packin' a lot of meat, but I wonder how long they'd last down in the short grass country. Them Texas ticks would eat 'em up alive."

"Yup. If they had to live on mesquites and soapweeds they wouldn't look so good, but some day we're all gonna be breedin' beefier cattle."

"It's the Texas ticks that make these Kansas farmers mad. They think the ticks make their cattle sick."

"They could be right, but our herd is far enough away, and there's enough country around here that I

127

don't believe they've got anything to worry about."

"Naw. And the ticks don't live through the winter anyhow. Hell, when the weather turns cold, there won't be any ticks."

"And we'll be gone by then."

"I'd still like to see their ranch."

"Yeah."

They rode on, eyes constantly watching the horizon. Not wanting to be accused of any mischeif, they went around the cattle. When they came to a creek they slid their horses down a steep bank and rode up a bank on the far side. A mile on they saw the first house. It was only a one-room sod shack with grass growing out of the dirt roof, but it could be shelter from the winter storms. The two riders studied it, saw no sign of life. A half mile farther they came to a dry ravine, and another man-made shelter. It was dug into the side of the ravine, with sod bricks sealing up the front. There was a door frame but no door. No sign of life either. Skirting it, they rode on until they topped a low hill and saw the ranch below them. There, there were a sod house and a big two-story house made of lumber. Smoke came from a chimney at the big house. There were a small barn made of rough lumber and four corrals. Horses stood in one of the corrals.

A man came out of the big house and started toward the barn. He saw the two riders a quarter mile away, stopped, then turned and ran back to the house. Two more men came out of the house and another came out of the barn. They stood in the yard and watched the riders. Will and Clint watched them.

Finally, Clint said, "They're ready to fight but I don't b'lieve they're lookin' for a fight today."

"Don't seem to be. Well, we ain't here to start a fight." Will turned his horse around and rode off the hill. Clint followed.

When they passed the dugout shelter and the sod shack, Clint said, "Don't look like nobody lives in 'em. Wonder if anybody ever did."

"I doubt it. You know about the homestead laws, Clint? Well, the way I heard it some eastern financier paid a bunch of men to claim a hundred and sixty acres apiece, and they put up those shacks so they could say they proved up on their claims. I heard they've got several sections here."

"Then we're on their land."

"Yup. We've got no right here. Let's lope."

Continuing south, they soon saw Dodge City sitting on the plains and the railroad running east. On the other side of the railroad was the Arkansas.

"Tell you what, Clint. I'd sure like to see if the railroad has started building a shippin' pen. Let's go have a look-see, but we can't stay."

"I got my fill of town yesterday, but when we get the cattle loaded, I'll have another fill."

"There's some side tracks on the west side. I'm guessin' that's where they'll build the pens."

He'd guessed right. When they rode up they saw that the planks and posts had been unloaded from the flatcar, and four men were digging postholes. They were just west of the livery barn, between the railroad and the river.

"That's a sight for sore eyes," Will allowed. "Lucas'll be mighty happy to hear about that."

Looking over at the livery barn, Will saw the short owner sitting on a bench outside, and reined his horse in that direction. But before they got there, the marshal walked out of the barn, leading a black horse. Immediately, Clint Overhart bristled.

"There's that cocky little rooster. He thinks ever'body oughtta jump when he hollers frog."

"Never mind him. Just pay him no mind."

At the barn, Will said, "Howdy, Mr. Easton. Hot enough for you?"

"It's hot enough for the devil hisself. See they're puttin' up some stock pens over there."

129

"Yeah, that's good news. When did they start, just this mornin'?"

Before he could answer, the marshal cut in. "You Texans got anything to do with that?"

"Why, yeah, I believe we have," Will answered.

"You think you're gonna ship cattle from here?"

"Yes sir, that's what we're gonna do."

The marshal still carried his six-gun in a holster tied low, and his right hand was always near it. He was clean shaven except for the bushy mustache. His badge was pinned on the front of his shirt. He looked at the ground, at the workmen, at the horizon, and back at Will. "I guess you're within the law, but I want to tell you, you cowboys better keep out of trouble in Dodge City. I don't want no more of that hollerin' and stompin' like we had last night."

Clint Overhart was still bristling. "We never bothered nobody. You're the one wanted a fight."

"I'm warning you."

The two men glared at each other until Will stepped between them. "We're goin' on back to the wagon now. Nobody's lookin' for trouble."

"Just remember what I said." With that, the marshal turned, got on his horse, and rode away north, back stiff.

"Don't start no ruckus with him," the livery owner advised. "Ever' day he goes over that hill up north and pops off a dozen shots from that hogleg he carries. He practices drawin' it fast and shootin' fast, and he's just lookin' for a chance to show ever'body how tough he is."

"Every day, huh?" Will asked.

"Purt' near. I c'n hear 'im from here. Some days he's gone all day."

"Shit." Clint Overhart's face was a mixture of anger and disgust. "Sooner or later me and that sumbitch're gonna tangle."

Chapter Sixteen

Sitting in the one chair in her room at the Dodge House, Lucina Mays weighed her chances—and the possibile consequences. Her brothers had both looked for that ravine and given up. She'd looked once and had to give up. The map was little if any help. If she went looking again, she could be spotted by some unfriendly Indians and killed. The Comanches and Cheyennes had a reputation for hating white women and children as much as they hated white men. They'd kill her without hesitation and cut off her scalp. Her body would be left to the prairie wolves. Her family would never know what had become of her.

So, go back to Kansas City? And do what? Marry some pudgy-faced young man in a stiff collar, with polish on his shoes? There was no one like Will Porter in Kansas City. Besides, she wanted to see those Texas cattle loaded on railcars and sent east. She could be proud of having a hand in it. It was something she'd arranged herself. Well, no, her grandfather Rathman did put in a word for her. But it was her idea and she'd done the selling. And it looked like it was going to work out just fine. She wanted to see it all happen.

And thinking of Will Porter gave her an idea. Maybe . . . No, he wouldn't. Couldn't. He was needed with the herd. Or was he? It would be a few days, maybe longer, before the shipping pens were built and the railcars would be available. Maybe if she told him the whole story and quit being so secretive, he'd be happy to go along.

After thinking about it all night, she decided that was what she would do. Now she had to get in touch with Will Porter. If she rode out to the Porter camp again, the cowboys would think she was crazy. Will Porter and his uncle would think she was crazy. Everyone in Dodge City already thought she was strange.

Well, if that was the only way she could contact the young cowboy she'd ride out to the cattle camp. But she'd wait a day or two and hope he came to town.

"Maybe you oughtta take another look at what the railroad's doin'," Lucas Porter said to his nephew. "With four men workin' it won't take long to build a big corral."

"I'm more worried about the stock cars," Will said. "I know the pens are bein' built. We've gotta have cars to ship cattle."

"And I've been thinkin' too about findin' a buyer. One of us'll have to go to Wichita or Kansas City and find a buyer for these beefs."

"Well, uh, you've had more experience with that than I have, Lucas."

"Time you got some experience."

They were scraping their breakfast plates. Lucas Porter dropped his in China Eye's washtub and walked away toward the remuda, spurs ringing. Will porter waited until he was out of earshot before he let out a long groan. What did he knew about selling cattle? What did he know about business? What were cattle worth on the market? He hadn't heard anything about that for months. Hell, a savvy cattle buyer would skin him alive.

But Lucas Porter had spoken, and that was that.

132

The big pen was already two-thirds built, and the men were building an adjacent smaller corral. They hadn't started on the loading chute yet, but that wouldn't take long. Still no cars, though. Will wondered if Lucina had heard anything new about the cars. It was an excuse to go see her. If she was still in town.

The horse he was riding was a little "boogerish," as the cowboys put it, and he didn't trust it to stand tied to the hitchrail, so he left it in a pen at the livery barn. Walking, spurs ringing on the planks, he started to pass the Longbranch, when he almost bumped into a burly man coming out.

"Whups," said Will.

"Whups, hell." The man did a double take—and grinned. "Wal, I'll be damned if it ain't the cowboy. What're you doin' in civilization? Still got that little pea gun?" He held out his hand to shake. He had a bushy black beard and he smelled.

Will shook with him. "How's huntin'? How long did you stay at Adobe Walls?"

"Hell's hooks, let me buy you one. Come on in here. I heered you got a herd of Texas longhorns over west of town."

Inside the Longbranch, Will took a sip of whiskey while the buffalo hunter downed his in one gulp. To be sociable, Will ordered another round. Only two other men stood at the bar, but two of the tables in the rear were occupied. "Yeah, we've got twenty-eight hundred head, minus one that we gave to some starvin' Indians. Findin' any buffalo?"

"Naw. It was a good deal for a few years, but word got around and ever'body and his damn brother came out here to git in on it. I was down in Texas for a while, and the shootin's scarce down there too."

"What're you gonna do?"

"I'm goin' down on those Staked Plains in Texas. That's where old Quahnah is, I reckon, but that's where

133

the buffler are too. If I c'n git enough men and guns together that's where I'll go."

"Some day there won't be any buffalo at all."

"Yeah." The hunter grinned a wry grin inside his black beard, showing tobacco-stained teeth. "Then I reckon I'll find me a woman and homestead a piece of land somewhere. Damned shame when a man has to make an honest livin'."

Chuckling, Will said he had to go see someone about some railcars. He wished the hunter good luck and turned to go. That was when he saw the bulldog again.

The husky man in overalls and jackboots came through the door with two other men. They were men who had threatened the Double O camp with shotguns. Bulldog had a red scar over his left eye and a lump on the left side of his jaw. He had to wear his floppy hat high on his head to keep it off the scar. When he saw Will he stopped suddenly.

Will groaned, "Oh-o-o no. Not now."

"Now, you lilly-livered daisy sonofabitch. Right now." Bulldog had another six-gun that looked exactly like the one Will had taken from him. His right hand hovered over it. "I'll give you a chance. Go for your gun."

Some chance. Bulldog's pistol was right at his fingers in a low-cut holster. Will's pearl-handled .44 was high on his hip in a deep holster. He had no chance.

"Just a goddam minute." It was the handsome bartender talking. "No shooting in here. If you have to kill each other go outside."

The buffalo hunter spoke next. "I take it these gents ain't friends of yours, cowboy."

"No," Will said. His eyes were on Bulldog's gun hand. His mind was racing, trying to find a way out. There was no way out.

"I cain't stop you two from fightin'," the hunter said, "but I'll keep these other two off of you." He had no gun, but he had a long-bladed skinning knife in a belt

134

sheath. He stepped up to Will's side, his hand on the knife handle. "Me and this cowboy have fought side by side before."

The barkeep pleaded, "Go outside, will you."

Bulldog said, "It's me and him. When he goes out he gits carried out. I'm givin' you a chance, Texas. Grab your gun."

Will's heart was beating too fast, too loud. No way out. No way. Grab the .44 and hope. No, that would be suicide. What then?

He stepped up close to Bulldog and tried to keep his voice strong. "What's happened between you and me you started. I never bothered you till you shoved a shotgun in my face." He got closer.

"All right, I gave you a chance." Bulldog's hand was a blur. It was filled with the six-gun. The hammer was back. Will's left fist came up from his knees. The fist connected with Bulldog's right eye at the same time the six-gun fired.

A sudden, searing pain in his left side staggered Will back a step. But while he was staggering his hand went to the Russian .44. He yanked it out of the Slim Jim holster and thumbed the hammer.

Bulldog was shaking his head to clear it after the blow to the eye. He had the six-gun cocked again.

Will's gun bucked with a loud pop. Bulldog pitched back. His six-gun went off, but the bullet drilled a splintery hole in the floor. He fell onto his back and lay still.

For a moment, everyone was quiet. The smell of burned gunpowder filled the room. Then the hunter warned Bulldog's partners, "Don't do it. I'll stick this knife in your gizzards."

The searing pain had Will doubled over. He dropped the .44 into its holster and put his right hand on the wound in his left side. Blood was soaking through his shirt. He walked, bent over, grimacing with pain.

"Where's the doc?" the hunter asked. "I heered

135

there's a doc in this town."

"Just around the corner east," the barkeep answered. "Goddam it, now that sonofabitch marshal's gonna be raisin' hell in here."

One day was as long as she was going to wait, Lucina Mays decided. If Will Porter didn't come to town today she was going to saddle her horse in the morning and go out to the cattle camp. Meanwhile, she decided to go to the livery barn and see to her horses. Mr. Easton had always taken good care of them, and she trusted him, but she liked horses and liked to handle them. Besides, Mr. Easton had always treated her like a lady and didn't stare at her when she wore men's clothes. Visiting with Mr. Easton would be a pleasant way to pass time.

She was walking in an ankle-length dress past the Longbranch Saloon when she heard the gunshots.

At first she hurried past the door, fear in her throat. But once past, she paused, curious. She heard someone yell, "Where's the doc?", and she heard boots clomping on the wooden floor toward the door. Staying back out of the way, she watched. Then she sucked in her breath and her blood turned cold.

It was Will and he was wounded.

"Oh my Lord," she muttered as she hurried to him. "What happened?" To the hunter, she said, "How bad is he? How . . . ?"

Will answered through his teeth, "Not bad, Lucina. Lu. I'm able to walk."

"Let me help you. There's a man around the corner who is supposed to be a doctor. Let's get him over there."

With the hunter's shoulder under his right armpit and Lucina Mays on his left, he walked around the corner and across a vacant lot to a small frame building. A sign in front read Chas. C. Plougher

MEDICINE. It didn't say doctor.

The bearded hunter banged on the door with a hard fist, and the door was opened by a little man in a long gray linen coat, a goatee, and thick eyeglasses.

"Are you a doctor?" Lucina asked.

"Well, I'm . . ."

"He's been shot," the hunter said.

"Bring him in here." The little man stepped back and motioned toward a cot on the far side of a plain room. A glass case full of medical instruments and bottles sat near the door.

"I don't need to lay down," Will insisted. He started unbuttoning his shirt, then glanced at Lucina and stopped, embarrassed.

"Oh, for heaven's sake, Will, do I have to turn my back?"

"Uh, well." He pulled his shirttail out of his pants and examined the wound himself. A red streak cut across his left side just above the waistband of his pants. It burned like fire. Lucina and the hunter stepped closer to examine it themselves.

"Since you-all are in my clinic, do you mind if I take a look?"

They stepped back to make from for Chas. C. Plougher. He adjusted his glasses and put his face close to the wound. "Would you lie down, sir? I can see it better if you lie down."

Glancing again at Lucina, Will turned, got his boots on the cot, and lay back. "Uh-huh," the little man said. "Turn over please." Will squirmed onto his stomach. "Well, it seems the bullet passed through the flesh, but hit no vital parts. You won't need surgery."

"Thank God," Lucina said.

"You're a lucky young man. An inch further and the bullet would have lodged inside and it would take surgery to remove it."

"Good," Will said. He turned over onto his back and tried to sit up. Pain brought a grimace to his face.

"Lie still, Will," Lucina said. "Let Mr. Plougher do whatever he thinks should be done."

"Not much I can do. I've got some carbolic soap here, and I'll heat some water and wash the wound. If it's kept clean it should heal nicely." The little man busied himself at a small cast-iron stove in one corner of the room, stuffing in some wrapping paper, then some kindling, and then some larger chunks of wood. He struck a match and started it burning.

The bearded hunter spoke. "Yeah, cowboy, looks like you're gonna live to brag about it."

"Brag about what?"

"About what? Why you just kilt a tough sonofa— excuse me, lady—a tough sonofabuck. He's always startin' fights. Was, I mean."

"Killed him?" Another groan came out of Will. "Lordy, lordy, I never killed a white man before. I was hopin' I never would."

"If you didn't he'd of kilt you. That was plain enough for ever'body to see."

"Oh, gaw-ud." Will sat on the edge of the cot and put his face in his hands.

That was when the door burst open and the marshal stomped in.

The little man with a badge and a big pistol marched straight to Will, put his right hand on his gun butt, and said, "You're under arrest."

"Huh? Why?" Will looked up with a pained expression at the marshal.

"For murder. I knowed you Texas cowboys would kill somebody. I warned you."

"Now just a minute, Marshal." Lucina Mays had a frown wrinkle between her hazel eyes. "This gentleman here said it was self-defense. He had to kill or be killed."

"Shore was," the hunter said.

"Sure. That's what every killer says." The marshal reached down for Will's right arm. "You're goin' to the lockup."

"No he is not." Lucina was so angry she was shaking. "A man has a right to defend himself. Besides he needs medical treatment. Get your hands off him or I'll . . . so help me, I'll make you sorry. I'll make you the sorriest son of a . . . son of a . . . there is."

"You're interfering with the law, young lady. That's a crime around here."

"Law, huh? We'll see what the law is."

Water was boiling in a tin pan on the stove now, and Chas. C. Plougher brought the pan over to the cot. "Step back, please. Let me do my work."

Reluctantly, the marshal gave him room, but glared at Will. "No matter what, you're goin' to the lockup."

"Would you lie down on your right side, please?" Plougher had a washcloth and a bar of yellow, smelly soap. When Will lay back, he lathered the cloth and began washing the wound. "This will prevent infection. Then we'll put a clean bandage on it."

Lucina said, "There's a police judge in Dodge City. I'm going to pay him a visit. Don't move him until I get back." Locking eyes with the marshal, she added. "You move him and I'll get the sheriff to arrest you for something. You can bet on that."

"The sheriff's out to his house with a busted leg. He ain't gonna arrest nobody. And the judge, he ain't t'home. He's somewheres tryin' to catch fish out of the Arkansas."

"Then I'll get a U.S. Marshal if I have to go clear to Wichita to do it." With that, Lucina Mays spun on her heels and walked rapidly out the door.

Chapter Seventeen

She no more than got outside than she realized she'd made a mistake. The judge would want evidence. She had to have evidence to present. That buffalo hunter in there was a witness to the shooting. Witnesses were good evidence. She'd have to go back inside and persuade him to go with her to see the judge. But if she couldn't find the judge, then what? A written statement? Yes, while the buffalo hunter was still in town she'd better get his statement in writing. Hunters came and went. He could leave any time. And while she was getting a written statement from him she'd better get written statements from other witnesses.

Half running, she went to her room at the Dodge House, grabbed her pad of paper and a pencil, and hurried back to the sidewalk and the medical clinic. Inside, Will Porter was sitting on the cot with his head in his hands, and the marshal was standing over him with a hand on his gun butt.

"Where's the gentleman who was here," Lucina asked, nearly out of breath. "The one with the black beard?"

Speaking over his shoulder, the marshal said, "I don't know and don't care."

Sarcastic now, Lucina said, "Thank you very very much."

"You better watch your mouth, young lady. I don't have to take no guff from nobody."

"Aw go to . . . go to hades." Lucina whirled and went out the door.

All right, she said to herself, all right, calm down. Be calm and think. You need statements from witnesses, right? Where would you find them? Only in the Longbranch Saloon where the shooting happened. That's no place for a lady. The only women who go in there are the, uh, soiled doves. Soiled doves, hell, the whores. If I go in there I'll be stared at again.

I'm going in there.

Determined, she walked with rapid steps to the plank walk and turned toward the door of the Longbranch Saloon. At the door she paused a moment; then, her chin up, she stepped inside.

The saloon was crowded now. Men were talking about the shooting. Talking and drinking. Lucina wasn't noticed at first. Then a red-faced railroad worker in suspenders spotted her. He did a double take and stared. Others saw her. The talking stopped.

"Uh, uh . . ." Lucina couldn't help it, she stammered. then she raised her chin again and blurted, "I'm looking for witnesses to what happened in here."

Someone said, "You are? How come?"

"Mr. Porter has been placed under arrest for murder, and I've been told the shooting was purely in self-defense. Did any of you see what happened?"

"Are you a sure 'nuff lady lawyer?"

"No, but I am working in Mr. Porter's defense. Did any of you see the shooting?"

"That 'un did." The railroader nodded toward the handsome bartender.

"Sir, did you see what happened?"

Before the bartender could answer, the black-bearded buffalo hunter stepped out of the crowd. "This here lady's my friend, and I'll thank you all to treat her with respect." To Lucina, he said, "I saw it. Just tell me

141

what you want me to do."

"I would like to get it in writing, what you saw and what you heard."

Someone laughed, "Bet he cain't write."

"Then I'll write it as you tell it." Lucina held her pad in one hand and her pencil in the other.

The hunter started, "Well, uh, we was havin' a friendly drink of whiskey and . . ."

Twice she had to stop him while she caught up, but she got it all down. "Would you sign this, please?"

"Shore." She handed him the pad and pencil, and he scrawled something illegible.

"Thank you very much. Now, who else? You, sir?" She was looking at the bartender.

"Yes, ma'am. I saw it. It happened the way he told it."

"Would you tell me again in your own words please?"

Within thirty minutes she had signed statements from three witnesses. Now she could get out of here. "Thank you all very much. You've been perfect gentlemen. Thank you."

"Haw, haw, come back any time little—huh?" The spokesman said no more when he was poked in the ribs.

Now, Lucina said to herself when she reached the sidewalk, I've got to find that judge.

His legs were a little unsteady but getting stronger when Will Porter buttoned his shirt and tucked the tail inside his pants. His wound was covered with a clean white bandage held in place by a thin strip of white cloth wrapped around his waist. The marshal had Will's pearl-handled .44 in his left hand. His right hand was on the butt of his own gun.

"I'd like to get word to my uncle at the wagon. He'll wonder what became of me."

"You should of thought of that before you started busting caps in my town."

Chas. C. Plougher handed Will the bar of yellow soap. "Wash with this twice a day. It should heal nicely."

"Fine. I'm much obliged. How much do I owe you?"

"Oh, two dollars will do, and fifty cents for the carbolic soap. I'm not a licensed doctor, you know, but I was a doctor's helper in a hospital in Abilene. Two dollars will be fine."

"Here, and I thank you." Will peeled two paper dollars off a roll he carried in his pants pocket.

"Start walkin', mister." The marshal pushed Will toward the door.

But just as they got there, the door was slammed open and Lucina Mays stood in it. Beside her was a tall, thin man in a finger-length dark coat, with a string necktie around his throat, and wearing a stovepipe hat. He was so thin he looked like a strong wind would blow him over, but he carried himself straight, shoulders square, dignified.

"This," Lucina Mays said, "is the prosecuting attorney, the Honorable James Maxon."

"Marshal," the attorney said, "I understand you are placing this man under arrest."

"Yeah. He shot and killed a man in the Longbranch Saloon."

"I have written statements here attesting to the fact that he acted in self-defense."

"Well, uh, that hasn't been proved. It's what he says."

"Have you interrogated witnesses?"

"Uh, no, not yet."

"When do you plan on doing that?"

"As soon as I get him locked up."

"Young man," the prosecuting attorney turned his gaze on Will, "you will have to go with the marshal to the jail. Arresting you on suspicion of committing a

143

felony is within the law. However, unless he can find evidence refuting the statements I have here I will decline to charge you with a crime and you will be released."

Lucina was shocked. "He has to go to jail? Even with the evidence I took to you?"

"If the marshal has reason to suspect him of a crime he should be signed into jail. However . . ."—the tall, thin man pulled a gold watch out of a vest pocket, glanced at it—"it is now eleven a.m. If the marshal has uncovered no evidence that would warrant a formal charge by four o'clock, I will suggest that the prisoner be released. Judge Wilson always goes along with my suggestions."

"This is outrageous." Lucina was shaking with anger again.

"I am sorry, madam, that is the law."

To Will, she said, "I'll do everything I can, Will. You won't be in jail long. I'll get my horse and go and find the judge."

"You've done a lot, Lu. Don't worry about me." He tried to smile. "Right now I feel lucky to be alive."

"Let's go." The marshal had his left hand on Will's right arm, and his right hand on the gun butt.

Lucina and the tall, thin attorney stood back as Will was marched through the door and out into the bright sunlight. On the plank walk, the marshal strutted like a bantam rooster as he marched his prisoner to jail. Town people stepped aside and watched, curious. At the end of the two-block walk, Will was led down a dirt side street, around a corner, and up to a two-room building. He realized he had been marched a block out of the way. The marshal had to show the town he was doing his duty.

The building was made of thick lumber and there were bars on the windows. The first room inside was the marshal's office. It contained a desk, two chairs, a wall covered with wanted posters, and another wall with a gun rack, a rifle, and a shotgun. A door made of steel bars connected it to the back room.

"Now, take off that gun belt and take everything out of your pockets. I hope you give me some trouble so I can lay this gun barrel upside your head."

Jaws clamped shut, Will did as he was told. Inside the jail cell, he sat on a wooden bunk with no matress or blanket and put his chin in his hands. The wound in his left side ached. He sat that way for an hour or so, then lay back on the bunk. His Stetson was his pillow. If he wasn't back at the wagon by dark, his uncle would come to town to look for him. What would Lucas do? Pay his fine if there was one, or try to bribe the judge? Some judges could be bribed, some couldn't. Or maybe Lucina would find the judge, or maybe that prosecuting attorney would keep his word and have him released.

His thoughts switched to the man he'd killed. A white man. He wondered if the bulldog-like man had a wife somewhere, or children. Or a mother. Why did it happen?

His side ached.

No lunch was served at noon, but he didn't expect nor want any. The marshal left at noon and didn't come back. Will stood and paced the wooden floor. The ache in his side was down to a dull burn now. He was tempted to take off the bandage and look at it, but he didn't.

In another hour he knew how caged animals felt. Helpless. Couldn't move more than a few feet, couldn't see out, couldn't talk to anyone, couldn't do anything but just sit and wait.

An hour later he was even more restless. Sitting still was impossible. He paced and swore. He felt like yelling. He wished the damned marshal would come back so he could ask what time it was. No, he wouldn't ask the damned marshal anything. Paced. Swore. Where was Lucas? Had he heard about it yet? No, not yet. He wouldn't suspect anything until dark. How long till dark?

The ache in his side was forgotten now. Swearing, he grabbed two of the bars in the cell door and tried to shake them. The were solid. He kicked at the door. Stomping across the cell, he kicked at the bunk. Back at the door he tried again to rattle the bars.

The outer door opened.

It was the tall, thin attorney who came in, stooping to keep from bumping his stovepipe hat on the door frame. The marshal was right behind him, almost hidden by him. Behind the marshal was Lucina Mays. "Don't fret," the tall, thin one said. "You are going to be released now. Unlock the door, marshal."

"Aw shit. What's the use locking up these rounders if you're gonna turn 'em loose." Still grumbling, the marshal took a long key from his hip pocket and approached the cell.

Lucina stepped around the attorney to where she could see Will. "Are you feeling all right? How is your wound?"

"I'm fine. Or, I will be as soon as I get out of here."

"Shit."

The attorney scolded, "That's no way to talk in front of a lady."

"Lady, hell. Ever'body in the Longbranch knows her."

"Yes," Lucina snapped, "and they know you didn't even try to question witnesses. You don't care. All you want to do is lock someone up."

"Aw shit." The door was unlocked and swung open.

Now Will knew how a caged animal felt when it was freed. He wanted to run and jump. He wanted to yell like a Comanche. Instead, he said, "Thanks, Lu. And thank you, sir." He held out his hand to shake with the attorney.

"You'll be back," the marshal said. "You and your whole damned crew. I'm just waitin' for one of you

146

Texans to shoot off your mouth. You'll be back. Or dead."

Lucas Porter took the news calmly. "Too bad," he said as he rolled a cigarette. "We made enemies just by bein' here. The sheriff's got a busted leg, you said?"

"That's what I heard."

"He won't be no help then." He struck a match with his thumbnail, set fire to his smoke, and watched his recently unsaddled horse roll on the ground to scratch its sweating back. "Are you scared to go back to town?"

"I can't be. Can't let that mean little sonofabitch scare me out of doin' business."

"Yup, and we've got business to do. When do you want to go to Wichita and find a cattle buyer?"

"No hurry. We can't ship cattle yet, and like you said they're gettin' fat on this free grass."

"That's right, but sooner or later one of us'll have to go."

"Yeah, I'll go if you don't want to. In a few days."

"How's that bullet wound?"

"It's all right." Will cracked a smile. "I only feel it when I breath."

"Reckon you'll have to quit breathin', then."

Chapter Eighteen

She had news. Exciting news. The kind of news that couldn't wait. No telling when Will Porter would come back into town. Not until he had to, that was certain. So she would go to him.

"Mornin', Miss Mays. Goin' for a little ride?"

"Yes, Mr. Easton. I don't expect to be gone long."

The livery owner was raking manure out of one of his corrals. He stopped, shoved his floppy hat back, and wiped his sweating forehead with a shirtsleeve. "Goin' out to that cowboy camp?"

"Yes. They are perfect gentlemen, those cowboys."

"How's the one that got in the shootin' match? Is he still kickin' around?"

"I believe so. I hope so."

"Wal, be careful, Miss. Never heard of a woman bein' attacked around here, but be careful. Let that bay horse head for the barn and he can prob'ly outrun most other horses."

Smiling, she said, "Yes, he does walk faster toward home." After pulling the latigo tight and buckling it in the cinch ring, she mounted and sat astraddle. She had ridden sidesaddle in Kansas City, but she was more comfortable astraddle the horse. And why shouldn't she be comfortable?

"If you ain't back by sundown we'll come lookin'

148

for you."

"I appreciate that, Mr. Easton, but it won't be necessary." She touched the horse with the heels of her shoes and rode away west.

If she had arrived earlier she would have had a long wait. The only human she saw at the Porter wagon was the cook, the man they called China Eye. He stopped what he was doing on the folding tailgate of the chuck wagon and watched her ride up.

"Good morning, sir."

"Mornin', Miss, uh . . ."

"Mays. Lucina Mays. Is Mr. Porter here?"

"I expect it's Will Porter you want to see. He rode off early this mornin', but I think he'll be back purty soon." He wiped his hands on a dirty apron, looked to the north, and added, "Here comes the remuda. Lucas told the hoss wrangler to bring 'em in about noon. That's a purty good sign they expect to be back about noon."

Lucina followed his one-eyed gaze and saw the herd of saddle horses being driven toward them. "Do you mind if I wait?"

"No, ma'am. Not a-tall. Git down and rest your saddle. I've got the coffeepot on."

She dismounted among the rolled-up canvas-wrapped cowboy beds. "Thank you very much."

China Eye continued working, pummeling a batch of bread dough and rolling it flat with a rolling pin. Now and then he stole a glance at her. Then, looking to the west, he said, "They're comin'."

Lucina saw five riders and when they came closer she recognized Will Porter and his uncle Lucas among them. All five stopped their horses fifty feet away from the wagon and Will exclaimed, "Lu. What brings you out here again?"

Lucas Porter said, "Howdy, Miss Mays."

The cowboys unsaddled their horses and pretended not to look at Lucina, but they couldn't help sneaking glances.

149

"I've got news," Lucina said. "The cattle cars are here."

"They are? That's good news." Will pulled the saddle off his mount and turned it loose.

"How many cars, Miss Mays?" Lucas Porter asked.

"I counted twenty. I hope that's enough."

With a wry grin, Will said, "No, I'm afraid that's not enough. Did this Mr. Littleton promise more than that?"

"Yes. The last time I talked to him he said more would be coming. How many do you need?"

"Darned if I know. I ain't seen a cattle car and I don't know how many cattle they'll hold. Maybe if I took a look at 'em I could make a guess."

"How is your wound, Will?"

"Oh, it's a lot better. Be as good as new in a few days."

"Will," Lucas Porter said, "go on back to town with her and make an estimate of how many cars we'll need. Then try to wire that superintendent and let him know."

"All right, soon's we get the wrinkles out of our, uh, soon's we eat."

"If you don't mind eating off your lap, Miss Mays, you're welcome to fill a plate and help yourself."

She sat cross-legged on the ground and managed to balance a tiny plate on one knee while she cut up a small steak. It was tasty, and she hadn't realized how good red beans could be. "Hmm. Delicious. My compliments to the chef."

China Eye was so pleased that he strutted like a peacock between the fire and the tailgate of the wagon. "I've got a batch of spotted pup, Miss Mays. For dessert." When he saw the puzzled look on her face, he added, "It's not really a pup, it's raisin puddin'."

"Oh. Wonderful."

The cowboys were silent, not knowing what to say and afraid of saying the wrong thing.

After their meal, Will caught a fresh horse out of the remuda and told his uncle it could take a long while to get a reply to his telegraph. He might not get back until the next morning. Then he and Lucina rode side by side to Dodge City. On the way, she presented him with a proposition.

"And if we're successful," she concluded, "I'll give you a share, Will. How about, oh, say, twenty-five percent?"

"Well." He was hesitant. "I sure would like to, Miss Mays, but I've go to help sell and ship these cattle first. When that's done, I'll be glad to go with you. I sure owe it to you."

She tried to conceal her disappointment with a smile. "Don't feel that you owe me anything, Will. and it's Lu, remember?" They rode silently for a moment, then, "Oh yes, you will owe me a nickel a head. Isn't that what we agreed on?"

"Yeah," he grinned. "I might even add two cents bonus."

The twenty cars were there, sitting on a long side track near the newly built stock pens, but Will could see they were short cars. He guessed they would hold about twenty head apiece. He tried to do some mental calculating. "Let's see, at twenty head per car, it will take, uh . . ."

She finished for him, "One hundred and forty cars. That's more than a railroad engine can pull."

"Yeah. It's gonna be several train loads. There's lots of work to be done."

Leaving their horses at the livery barn, they walked to the railroad depot, where Will sent a telegraph to Hiram Littleton: "Need about 140 cattle cars," his telegram said. "When can you deliver? Please advise soonest. Signed Horace William Porter."

"Horace?" Lucina's eyebrows went up as she stood beside him at the long counter and read the message. She threw her head back and laughed. "Horace? What

151

do they call you for short, Ho—?"

Chuckling, Will said, "Go ahead. Just go ahead. Lucy."

Her laughter ended in a strangling sound. "Truce."

He waited in the hotel lobby while she went to her room and changed out of her man's clothes into a long dress that was pulled in at the waist with a cloth belt. After brushing her hair she went down and sat in a chair beside him. They were alone in the lobby.

"Now," Will said, "tell me more about your granddad."

Taking a careful look around to be sure no one else was within hearing distance, she began:

"Grandfather Mays was an entrepreneur, one of the adventurous kind, the kind I admire. He did some trading in Santa Fe. Three times he took a string of wagons loaded with trade goods over the Santa Fe Trail, and each time he made a profit. On his last trip, he sold his trade goods, wagons, and mules and paid off his teamsters. He started home alone. He . . ."

She stopped talking when two well-dressed men took chairs nearby. "Uh, Will, we can't talk here. Would you accompany me to my room?"

"Your room? Me? In your room?"

"Yes." She wore a no-nonsense expression. "We have business to discuss and we have no office. My room will have to do." Standing, looking at the two men, she dared them with her eyes to show any interest in the conversation. They were staring at her, but quickly looked away.

"Well, all right." Will stood, too.

Her room contained only one chair so Will stood just inside the door, his hat in his hands. He was embarrassed at being in such intimate surroundings with an attractive young lady. She sat on the edge of the bed, motioning him to the chair. He continued to stand.

"Won't you please sit down, Will. I'm the one who

152

should be embarrassed. I've never had a man in my room before." And then she realized the conversation was not going the way she wanted it to go. "I can talk to you better if you sit."

Finally he did, but on the edge of the chair, still holding his hat, both feet planted on the floor.

His embarrassment tempted her. She couldn't help it. She had to tease him a little. "Haven't you ever been in a room alone with a lady? Why, I would have thought a man of your worldliness would have been everywhere."

Stammering, "Uh, uh," his mind went to the saloon women and the women in San Francisco. With them in mind, in her presence, he was even more embarrassed. "Why, uh . . ."

"Ahum. Never mind. Don't answer that. It's none of my business. Now then, let's talk about real business."

"Yeah, yes. Your granddad."

"What I am telling you is what I heard from my father and brothers. Grandfather Mays thought it was not my concern." A wry smile touched her face briefly. "He thought I was a cute little girl and he liked to bring me presents, but he thought I should ignore men's affairs." She paused to see if Will was interested. He was still sitting on the edge of the chair, but he was listening intently.

"All right, he left Santa Fe alone, riding one horse and leading a packhorse carrying, well, let me back up a step, he wouldn't accept paper money, but he did accept silver specie. The coins could be redeemed easily in Kansas City. So the packhorse was carrying approximately one hundred and thirty pounds of silver."

"Whew." Will was beginning to relax. "That's what I'd call a load of money."

"We estimate that it is worth twenty thousand in U.S. government paper."

"I can believe it What happened?"

"He got across the Cimarron River and into Kansas when he was attacked by Indians. He rode for his life. I don't know how long the chase lasted, but Grandfather believed his packhorse, carrying a dead weight, could not outrace them all the way to Fort Dodge. He rode into a ravine and stopped to let his horses blow. It was there that he saw an arrow in his saddle horse's hip. He knew the horse could go no farther." Pausing again, Lucina swallowed, cleared her throat.

"Yeah?" Will was impatient, wanting her to go on with the story.

"He had to ride the packhorse, and that meant leaving the packs behind. It was either lose the silver or lose his life. The Indians apparently had lost sight of him momentarily, but he knew they would find him again. He quickly unloaded the packhorse and transferred his saddle from one horse to another. But, being a Mays, he couldn't just leave twenty thousand dollars worth of silver coins lying on the ground. He used a shovel he had and buried the packs. When he rode out of the ravine, he was seen by the Indians, and the race resumed. The Indians shot at him with guns and arrows.

"Fortunately, Grandfather's horse was grain fed and stronger than the Indians' horses. He outraced them to Fort Dodge. Once there, he discovered that he had been shot. The bullet entered his back on the right side, but in the excitement of the chase, he hadn't even felt it. An army surgeon removed the bullet, and Grandfather resumed his journey home. That was before the railroad had reached this far west, and he had to ride a horse to Wichita. From there, he traveled by rail the rest of the way to Kansas City. He felt lucky to be alive.

"But the wound in his back had not healed, and it was very painful. My father took him to a hospital where it was discovered that the wound had become terribly infected. Grandfather died a week later."

"Aw-w-w." Will was saddened.

Lucina stood, went to a pitcher of water on a table, and filled a drinking glass. She offered the glass to Will, and when he shook his head she drank from it and placed it on the table. Then she stood in front of him, hands on her hips.

"Now you know what I was doing by myself down there on the prairie."

"Yeah." He digested what she'd said, then asked, "But what about your dad and brothers? How come they didn't try to find it."

"They did, but they gave up. Grandfather drew a map, but it's not much help. I tried once and I failed too, I was hoping that you would . . . if a Mays doesn't find it Grandfather will have died in vain, and I was hoping that you would, when you have time of course, go back with me, and . . ."

"You bet." Will stood. "That's a lot of money. We'll go find it."

Chapter Nineteen

The answer to his telegram came after dark, after he and Lucina had dinner in the Dodge House restaurant. It said: "Sixty cars available approx Aug. 19. More later. Advise if still interested."

"Let's see," Will said, "sixty and twenty are eighty, and that means we will need sixty more. Today is, uh, August what?"

"That's only four days away, Will."

"Yeah, won't be long now."

They stood in the depot, alone except for the stationmaster. "Do you still want to ride south with me?"

"Sure. As soon as we get those cattle to Wichita. I'll have to take the train to Wichita tomorrow and try to find a buyer. It'd be better to have a buyer waitin' there for us than to have to look for a buyer after we get there."

"Of course. Then you won't be able to go with me for a week or so." It was a statement.

"I'm sure sorry, Lu. I'll go with you as soon as I can."

"Of course." She tried, but she couldn't conceal her disappointment.

*   *   *

After Will had ridden off in the dark for the Double O wagon, Lucina went to her room, feeling glum. If only Will didn't have to find a buyer they could be on their way south early tomorrow. She knew of a buyer. Should she tell Will about her conversation with Mr. Goodwin of Goodwin & Sons Livestock Co.? It could save him a trip.

No. She lay back on the bed and felt even gloomier. She'd had not business talking with Mr. Goodwin. She should stay out of it. Will and his uncle would want to conduct their own business in their own way. They wouldn't believe a twenty-two-year-old girl would be able to sell cattle. And besides, Will might find a buyer who would pay more than Mr. Goodwin.

No, she would have to resume her search on the prairie alone, or wait. She didn't want to wait.

But she wanted Will to go with her.

"We-el now," Lucas Porter mused when he and Will walked away from the chuck wagon and the cook's dying fire. "That's some tale. Twenty thousand, she said?"

"Yeah. That's a guess."

"And her dad and older brothers tried to find it and gave up?"

"Yeah."

"She's no quitter, that girl. Seems to me you owe her. Matter of fact, we both do. She's the one is gettin' those cattle cars and all."

"Yeah."

"And she worked purty hard to get you out of jail and out of trouble."

"Yeah."

"She didn't quit on you."

"No."

"Well, you ain't gonna quit on her, are you?"

157

"No, but . . ."

"I'll go to Wichita and find a buyer. You go with her."

"But you said . . ."

"Wal, I changed my mind. Catch a couple of good hosses in the mornin' and git gone."

Suddenly it felt as though an anvil had been lifted from Will's shoulders. A painful worry had been removed. He no longer had to be torn between two loyalties. He wanted to shake his uncle's hand, pat him on the back, do something, say something. But after thinking it over he said simply, "Thanks Lucas."

Lucina was eating breakfast alone in the Dodge House restaurant, still feeling gloomy. Her head came up sharply when Will Porter walked into the room. His boots thumped and his spurs chinged as he walked straight toward her.

"Say, Lu," he said, "you can't ride a horse in that getup, can you?"

"Why no. Why?"

"We've got a day and a half ride ahead of us and we're burnin' daylight."

"What? Do you mean . . . ?"

"Lucas is goin' to Wichita."

"Oh, Will." She stood so suddenly she knocked her chair over. He picked it up. "Will, give me fifteen minutes. No, make that ten minutes. I'll be right back."

They left Dodge City heading southwest, following the Santa Fe Trail, each riding one horse and leading another. Lucina had already bought a supply of groceries in preparation for the day she would go back and resume her search, and Will had brought some dried beef and biscuits from the Porter chuck wagon. Each packhorse carried two canvas panniers, a bedroll,

158

and a shovel. Their plan was to ride to the Cimarron crossing, then try to guess which way Lucina's grandfather had ridden when he was being chased by Indians.

Camp that night was in a wide draw where they couldn't be seen from any distance and where there was grass for the horses. Will gathered old buffalo chips for a fire, but didn't light them until after dark, hoping the smoke wouldn't be seen in the night sky. They roasted some fresh steaks over the fire, ate, and lay back on their spread-out beds.

"It does kind of give you the creepies, doesn't it Will, knowing there could be hostile Indians around."

"It does for a fact. I can't decide which is better, stayin' down here where we'd be hard to find or gettin' on top of this draw where we can see a long ways. If there's any Comanches around I'd like to see 'em comin'."

"I have to leave the decision up to you." She stood. "Would you excuse me, please?"

"Huh? Oh, sure." Boy, he thought as she walked away into the darkness, I'm about to bust a bladder. He walked in the opposite direction. This campin' with a girl is a hell of a note. A man can't take a pee when he feels like it. Somebody once said a woman can hold it longer than a man. She sure as hell can.

Back at the fire, he lay on his bed on his back with his hands under his head. It was a warm night, and the stars where thick in the sky. After a few minutes, he became worried, and sat up. "Lu?"

"I'm here. I'm not lost." Her voice came out of the dark. Then she appeared, not much more than a moving shadow on the other side of the dying fire.

She poured water from a canteen over her hands, one at a time, then sat on her bed. They were only fifteen feet apart. Neither spoke for a time. Will could hear the hobbled horses grazing nearby.

"Do they ever step on you?" she asked. "The horses?

159

When you're sleeping on the ground?"

"Never have. Came close to it once, but I woke up and scared him away."

"How did that happen?"

It was obvious she wanted to make conversation, and he felt like talking, too. "He was just curious. You know how horses are when they see somethin' they're curious about. First they smell of it, then they want to feel of it with their lips, and next they'll nip it with their teeth. Or if it's on the ground they might paw at it with a forefoot. Just to see what happens."

"Oh my."

"He had his nose in my face, and in another second or two he probably would have pawed at me."

"What did you do?"

"Just raised up. That scared him worse than he scared me, and he ran off."

The fire had died and it was dark. She chuckled at his story. He heard clothes rustling, or a blanket, or a bed tarp. Clothes? She wouldn't take her clothes off, would she? Some men couldn't sleep with their clothes on. Could she? He couldn't help thinking about it, trying to imagine how she would look with her clothes off. She had a good figure, he knew by the way she filled out her dresses. What would it be like to go over and lie down beside her? What would she do? There was nobody else around for miles. Just the two of them. Would she holler, beat at him with her fists? Or would she welcome him with open arms?

A weakness spread over his stomach, his knees. Just thinking about it made his heart beat faster. He had to find out? How? What to say?

"Lu?"

"Yes."

She was wide awake, maybe thinking the same thing. "Uh, Lu, uh, suppose we, uh, had only one bed. What would we do?" His pulse raced as he waited for an answer.

160

The answer came, clear and firm, "Then you would sleep on the ground, like the gentleman you are."

"Aw-w-w." He pulled off his boots and crawled under a blanket. "Aw-w-w."

"Good night, Will."

By sunup they were moving again, following the wagon wheel tracks that went to Santa Fe. At midmorning they passed two freight wagons loaded with buffalo hides going to Dodge City. The buffalo hunters whoaed their mule teams and talked a while. Yes, they had seen Indians two days earlier in the Texas Panhandle, but there were only a few and they kept their distance. The Cimarron was a half dozen miles behind them. They eyed Lucina curiously, trying to decide whether she was male or female. Finally, they churruped to their teams and went on.

In another half hour Will and Lucina came to the Cimarron.

They rode their horses into the water and let them drink, then Will went upstream and filled their canteens with brown water. "Won't taste good," he said, "but it'll wet your whistle."

"Now." Lucina dug her grandfather's map out of a jacket pocket. "We know—at least we can be reasonably—sure that Grandfather Mays crossed here. It wasn't far from here that the race began."

Looking over her shoulder at the map, Will allowed, "He'd probably head straight for Fort Dodge and that's a few miles on the other side of Dodge City."

"I think it's safe to assume that it's on this same trail."

"Probably is. Let's get horseback and ride along here and think about it. I do my best thinkin' on a horse."

After riding northeast for a mile, retracing their own route, Will reined up. "He didn't say, did he, which direction the Indians came from?"

Lucina pushed back her big hat. Her forehead was wrinkled in thought. "I don't think so. I don't recall

161

anyone mentioning that. It would make a difference, wouldn't it?"

"It sure would. Think. If we knew it might save us some time."

"I'm thinking. If they came from the east, he wouldn't keep going northeast, and if they came from ahead of him, he would turn and go back."

"The first time I saw you you were in an arroyo east of here."

"Yes, and I saw no sign of anything."

Shifting in his saddle, Will said, "He didn't go back. The river was behind him. And if the Indians came at him from the west, he'd keep goin' up this trail." Nodding toward the northwest, he added, "Unless they came from up there and could have headed him off. Then he'd go straight east. Let's have another look at that map."

Dismounted, they spread the map on the ground and squatted before it. Will put his knees on it to hold it down in the prairie breeze. "Huh," he grunted. "Plain as day. His X is east of this trail. He couldn't of got turned around, could he?"

"That's possible, but I don't think so. Not Grandfather Mays. That's why I was searching over east."

Standing, Will squinted across the prairie. "All right, let's go east and see what we can see. Somewhere within the next few miles, he quit the trail, loped down an arroyo, and hid."

"Yes. But he knew he couldn't hide there for very long."

"Well, we'll have to ride down every arroyo we come to."

They spent the rest of the day riding the length of five arroyos running east and west. Some of them were choked with brush, and that worried Will. "This brush could have grown here in the past ten years."

"That would make it almost impossible to find the packs, then."

162

"Not only that, we know it can rain terrible hard on the prairie. Water can run down these arroyos right after a rain and carry dirt and sand with it."

"Running water could erode the ground and uncover the packs," Lucina mused, "and the next rain could cover them again."

"All we can do is look. Look for anything unusual."

At times they got off their horses and poked through the brush, and once, when they came to a small depression in the sandy bottom of a ravine, they used the shovels to dig down several feet.

"He didn't have time to dig a deep hole," Will said. "No use tryin' to hit a Chinaman on the head with a shovel."

Lucina chuckled, "If we dig clear through the earth, we'll hit a Chinaman on the soles of his shoes. Wouldn't that make him hop."

"He'd jump clean out of those sandals the Chinamen wear."

"Sandals? Have you seen Chinese people?"

"Yeah, in San Francisco."

"You'll have to tell me about that."

"This hole's deep enough," he said, changing the subject. "Let's find some other place to dig."

At sundown they had to give up for the day. They went back to the Cimarron, where there was water, and camped for the night. Since talking to the two buffalo hunters, they were less worried about Indians.

"Where will we look tomorrow?" Lucina asked, gazing into their small fire.

"Darned if I know."

"It could be impossible to find."

"Somebody'll find it. I hate to think of some lucky jasper stumblin' over it by accident."

"Some day this will all be plowed land."

"What makes you say that?"

"The farmers are moving west. At present they think of the western prairie as wasteland, but eventually

163

they'll find a strain of wheat or corn that will grow here."

"It ain't wasteland." Will spoke a little sharper than he meant to. "It's good grassland. It would be a dirty shame to plow it up."

"I understand how you feel, Will, but men will use the land in whatever way is the most profitable."

"Yeah, I reckon. But it's a dirty shame."

"If I were in your place, I'd feel the same way."

He was silent, brooding about plowed ground, dirt blowing off plowed ground. He'd seen it in Texas, farmers tearing up the grass and trying to grow a crop where nothing not planted by nature would grow. She broke his mood. "Tell me about San Francisco. Have you actually been there?"

"Huh? Oh, yeah. Once. I set out to see the world." He told her about San Francisco and how glad he was to get away from there and back to Texas.

"Boy, you've traveled more than I have. I'll have to go out there some day."

"Like the feller says, it's somethin' to see, but don't stick around too long."

"Well, tomorrow is going to be our lucky day, Will, I can feel it in my bones. Good night."

Again, he heard the clothes rustling in the dark, and again his pulse quickened. "You don't think, we could, uh . . ."

"No. Not tonight. Not here."

"Aw-w-w."

Chapter Twenty

The sun came up right on schedule, hot and brassy. The prairie breeze hadn't let up a minute. A thin layer of clouds hung over the western sky, but there was no hint of rain. They were horseback, retracing their earlier route again. By midmorning heat waves created nonexistent lakes in the distance. They searched two ravines that were a half mile apart, and when they rode out of the second one, Will reined up.

"You know what bothers me?"

"What, Will?"

"Look at it this way, the Comanches were burnin' his tail, and he said he ducked down an arroyo and hid from 'em for a while. You couldn't hide a horse in these arroyos we've been searchin'."

Sliding off her horse, Lucina stretched her back and straightened her legs one at a time. "You're right. It doesn't seem possible that they wouldn't have seen him go into the ravine."

"We're in the wrong part of the country, Lu."

"Where else could he have gone?"

"Back yonder a ways those wagon tracks took a turn to the east to go around the end of an arroyo. Could it be he crossed the trail there and got west of it without knowin' it?"

"Hmm."

"If he had a bunch of screamin' Comanches behind 'im, he could have crossed the wagon tracks without seein' 'em."

"So you think we ought to be searching west of the trail?"

"We ain't doin' any good over here."

"All right." She mounted and followed him.

Two miles northwest, the terrain was rougher, with more low hills and a few small trees growing out of the draws. The ravines were plentiful.

"Does this look more likely, Will?"

"Does to me. How about you?"

"Is that a creek up ahead?"

"Don't know. There's trees and tall weeds. There had to've been water there some time."

It was a creek. Only a trickle of water ran down its sandy bottom, but they could see by the banks that the water had been higher and swifter at times.

"This has been one hot dry summer," Will allowed. "Only rained once since we left Texas. That one was a frog strangler, but it didn't take long for the water to soak in or run off." He dismounted and used one of the shovels to dig a shallow hole in the creek bed. Soon enough water that the horses could drink gathered in the hole. They loosened the cinches and let the horses graze while they ate dried beef and a can of peaches. Then they were mounted again.

By dark they were discouraged. They had ridden the length of four more ravines, dug four holes, and all they'd seen was sand, brush, gopher holes, and jackrabbits. They went back to the creek and camped for the night.

"This reminds me," said Will, after they'd eaten their fill of tinned beef and tomatoes, "of prospectin' for silver in the Black Mountains of southern New Mexico."

"You've done that too?"

A dry chuckle came from him. "Not for long. I

166

wouldn't have recognized that float, as they call it, if it bit me."

"You'll recognize silver specie when you see it."

"You still think we're gonna find it?"

"As you cowboys say, you betcher boots."

"Well, at least this sand is easier to dig in than those New Mexico rocks."

It was noon the next day when they found their first clue. Will had reined up sharply and dropped off his horse as if he'd fallen off.

"What happened, Will. You didn't fall off, did you?"

"Not likely. Come'ere."

"What is it? Oh, some bones. A piece of a skull? It's animal, isn't it."

"It's what left of a horse. This is a piece of the upper jawbone of a horse?"

"How do you know? Couldn't it have been a cow, or a deer or something?"

"Huh-uh. Cows ain't got any upper teeth in front. It was a horse."

"Oh. I see." She dismounted, too. "Do you suppose . . . could it have been . . ."

"The wounded horse your granddad left behind."

"Really?"

"Well, not for sure, but it could be. Trouble is, the wolves and coyotes would have scattered the bones far and wide." He stood and squinted into the heat waves.

"But perhaps it proves that we're in the right vicinity."

"Maybe."

"At least it gives us something to hope for."

Mounted again, he said, "Let's have a look in that arroyo over there."

It was about two hundred yards north, shallow at one end and deep in the middle. They rode slowly, carefully scanning the ground. Twice, Will dismounted, squatted, and scooped up dirt and sand with his fingers. Standing, looking around him, he said, "A

167

man could hide in here, all right."

"Yes. It's a likely spot."

But when they reached the other end they had seen nothing interesting. On they went, and soon they came to another ravine, another deep one. They rode the length of it, turned around, and rode back. Will said, "If the Comanches were lookin' for him in that arroyo back there while he was in this one, that would have given him a little time."

"Yes. This would be a good place to hide for a few minutes."

On foot again, Will walked and dragged the toes of his boots, digging furrows. In places the ground was soft sand, and in other places grass grew out of brown soil. "If I was to dig a hole and was in a hurry, I'd dig in the sand."

"A sandy hole would be easy to cover up too," Lucina said.

"But it could have changed in ten years."

Still dragging his feet, Will went on. Suddenly he stopped, kicked at something in the sand, squatted. Immediately, she was on the ground beside him. "What?"

With both hands he scooped sand away from a wooden object. Then they were both digging with their hands. In their excitement they forgot about the shovels. Then Will was pulling on something. It was two pieces of wood, crossed, with scraps of dried, twisted leather straps attached. He pulled it free. "A crossbuck saddle. A pack saddle like ours. It was his."

Lucina was so excited she was dancing. "It was grandfather's. This is the place. We've found it, Will."

"Let's get the shovels."

Within ten minutes, Lucina's shovel hit something hard. She squealed, "It's here, it's here. Will, this is it."

In another ten minutes they had dug up two pack panniers made of leather, now dried and hard, and inside the packs were at least a hundred and fifty pounds of silver Mexican coins.

"Gaw-ud damn," Will said, then added, "Excuse me, Lu."

"Gaw-ud damn is right." Lucina picked up handfuls of coins and let them slide through her fingers. "Have you ever seen so much money?"

"Not in my whole put-together."

"Whoo-ee."

Will climbed up to where he could see over the top of the ravine. Not another living creature was in sight. He slid back to the bottom on the seat of his pants. Lucina was in his arms, hugging him, squealing with excitement. "We did it. We found it. We're rich."

But it wasn't riches that was on his mind right then. She was in his arms, and in spite of the baggy, shapeless clothes, she was every inch a female. Her breath was sweet on his cheek. She was soft and cuddly and . . . without intending to, without thinking about it, he kissed her. Full on the mouth.

A squeal was cut short and she drew back. Her hazel eyes were fixed on his. A wrinkle appeared between her eyes. Then she returned the kiss, long and sweet. When she drew back this time, she smiled. He tried another kiss, but she put her fingers against his lips. "Not now, Will. Please."

"Gaw-ud damn."

The silver coins made a light load for their two packhorses, and they rode north until they came to another trickle of a creek. By then it was nearly dark, so they camped for the night.

"What are you gonna do with the money, Lu?" He was sitting cross-legged on the ground, eating tinned beef and corn. She was on the opposite side of a small fire.

"First thing I have to do is convert it to U.S government dollars. I don't know what the rate of exchange is, but I should have enough money here to open a business of some kind. How about you? Half of

169

it is yours."

"You said a quarter."

"That's what I said, but were it not for you neither of us would have it. Half is fair."

"I agreed to a quarter. Besides, it's somethin' your granddad left you."

"Are we going to argue, Will?"

"Yeah, if you insist."

"We'll discuss it later. Right now we have to get back to Dodge City. I might have to transport this specie to a bank in Wichita or Kansas City."

"Come to think of it I didn't see a bank in Dodge City."

"There is none, but Rath and Wright Mercantile has been acting as a bank. It was Mr. Wright who platted Dodge City. He and his partner seem to be honest. Perhaps I can deal with them."

"If you can, convert my one-quarter too. I'd rather carry paper money, now that it seems to be worth what it's supposed to be worth."

"U.S. government paper currency is acceptable and dependable now."

"We ought to get back to Dodge City late tomorrow. How are you gonna handle a load of coins?"

"We've got a problem, haven't we? I can, with your help, carry it up to my room at the hotel and find some way to carry it on the train. Hmm. It's going to be awkward. I suppose you'll keep yours at your cattle camp. It would be well guarded there."

"Yeah. Well, you can keep yours there too till you get ready to move it."

"May I? That would be better than carrying it up to my hotel room and piquing everyone's curiosity."

"Sure. I figure the wagon's straight north of here. Let's stop there first."

"What are you going to do with your share, Will?"

"That's something I'll have to think about. I, uh, I've got some money my folks left. I've been thinkin' about goin' into the cattle business on my own."

"You have the experience. And you know, Will, going into business is the smart thing to do. You could lose your shirt, of course, but there are men who invested everything in business and went broke, and . . . I can name at least two whom I know personally, my grandfather Rathman is one, who went broke, managed to scrape together a few dollars and went into business again. Eventually they became wealthy."

"It's like rollin' the dice, I reckon."

"Yes, but at least you have a chance. As long as you work for wages you have no chance."

"Can't argue with that. You said you're goin' into business—what kind of business? And where?"

"I've been giving a lot of thought to . . . well, actually, I haven't decided yet."

"You'll be goin' back to Kansas City?"

"Perhaps. Perhaps not."

"You don't know or you're bein' a mystery woman again?"

"I don't know just yet, Will. Honest, I don't."

"All right."

Silence. The fire sizzled and made muffled popping sounds as it burned dry limbs from one of the few small oak trees that grew along the stream. She excused herself and went off into the darkness. He went in the opposite direction. When he returned she was in her bed, only a dim form in the gloom. Pulling off his boots, he remembered that kiss back there in the ravine, and he ached for another. Did it mean anything? She liked him and trusted him. Was that all it meant?

"Lu?"

"Humph." She was half asleep.

Horseback again, they were eager to get back.

171

Lucina wanted a bath in a tub of hot water, and Will wanted to know whether his uncle had returned from Wichita and whether he'd found a cattle buyer. The country was flatter here, with only a few shallow ravines. Were it not for the tufts of bunchgrass and the gopher and badger holes, a man could shoot a game of pool on the ground. Heat waves danced ahead of them.

The sun was halfway down in the western sky when they saw the Arkansas ahead. A few minutes later they herd faraway gunshots.

"Uh-oh," Will said. "Somebody's shootin'."

"Who? Why?"

"The damned farmers, I'll bet." He snorted, "Farmers, hell, they're nothin' but hired gunsels. Let's lope."

Chapter Twenty-One

They rode at a gallop, leading the packhorses, until they were within two hundred yards of the river and the cottonwood trees. There, Will slowed to a walk, and Lucina slowed beside him. The gunshots were sporadic now, and Will guessed the gunsels were taking potshots at the Double O wagon and the men around it.

"You stay here," he said. "Probably everybody's on the other side of the river, but we can't be sure. Stay here and watch the horses."

"But I've got my rifle. I can shoot."

"No. Stay here. If I need you I'll holler, all right?"

Nodding, she said, "All right."

Afoot, he carried the Winchester in his left hand and the Russian .44 in his right. He half ran to the trees that grew along the riverbank, then crouched and walked carefully through the tall weeds to the river's edge. From there he could see the wagon and three men behind it, between it and the river. They had rifles and were looking to the north. A gunshot came from the north, then another. One cowboy squinted down his rifle barrel and returned the fire, quickly jacking another round into the gun's firing chamber.

It didn't make sense. Why would the gunsels stay back and fire a shot at the wagon now and then? What did they hope to gain by that? If the shooting continued, the rest of the cowboy crew would hear it and come at a run. It didn't make sense.

And then it did.

It was a shot from behind him that warned him. From far behind. Looking back, he saw Lucina point her long rifle in the air and fire again. A man cursed. He saw the men.

There were six of them, four in the water and two on the bank. One of the men on the bank wiped water off his face with the palm of his right hand and aimed a rifle at Lucina.

The Russian .44 popped, and the man dropped his rifle and fell onto his knees. Another man swore, "God damn it, there's some of 'em over here."

"God damn."

Will ducked behind a tree just as a bullet clipped bark off the side of it. He fired his six-shooter again at a man who waded out of the river and climbed onto the bank. Another bullet smacked into the tree.

Their strategy was obvious now. They intended to keep the cowboys at the wagon looking north while six of them waded the river and got behind them. There were six of them—five now—and only Will over here. He dropped to his knees to make himself harder to see, holstered the six-gun, and cocked the hammer back on the rifle. The five had disappeared. They were either in the tall weeds or behind the cottonwoods. They knew where he was but he couldn't see them. This wouldn't do at all.

Flat on the ground now, Will crawled backward, away from the tree and into the weeds. A shot, and a bullet thudded into the ground near his face. He'd been seen. Two more shots came his way and he could feel the heat of the bullets. If they kept shooting he'd be hit.

"Aw, no," he muttered under his breath. He didn't want to die. Not now. Not here.

Run. Run for the nearest big tree. He ran, wishing he'd taken the spurs off his boots. A bullet whined within two inches of his right cheek. He ran and dove headfirst behind a tree that grew on the edge of the river. A bullet plowed into the ground near his left shoulder and another tore splinters off the tree.

As fast as he could squirm, Will got onto one knee behind the tree. He looked for a target, saw movement in the weeds fifty feet ahead of him, threw the rifle to his shoulder, and fired. The movement stopped. But now bullets were flying at him from three directions, chipping the bark off the tree and fanning his face. They had him pinned and they were going to kill him.

A shot came from off in the distance, and for a few seconds the shooting along the riverbank ceased. Then a man yelled, "That jasper's still out there with some horses. Git the sonofabitch."

Lucina.

From behind his tree, Will saw another man stand and point a rifle in Lucina's direction. He aimed hastily, squeezed the trigger. The man pitched forward onto his face.

And then more shots came, fast and furious. Now they were coming from behind Will. Glancing back, he saw that the cowboys from the wagon were shooting from the opposite bank. Lead was flying back and forth across the river like a swarm of angry hornets.

"God damn it, git out of here."

"We can't. The horses are over there."

"There's that man out there with the horses, git 'im, git the horses." Three men crashed out of the weeds and ran, ran south toward Lucina.

"No you don't," Will muttered out loud. "No you sons of bitches don't."

He was running again, out of the weeds behind the three men, firing without taking aim, trying to divert their attention. Lucina saw the three running at her. She tried to get on her horse, but the animal was snorting and jumping at the gunfire. Will yelled, "Get down, Lu. Hit the ground."

175

She gave up trying to get on the horse and put the rifle to her shoulder. The rifle cracked.

The leader of the three fell so hard he slid on his face before his body came to a stop. The other two dropped their guns and threw up their hands. "Don't shoot. We give up. Don't shoot."

Out of breath, Will hurried up to them. "Get away from those guns. Get the hell away from them. Move, God damn it, or I'll drop you right there."

They moved, stepped back, kept their hands in the air, their eyes fixed on the bore of Will's rifle. Two cowboys came running up, clothes wet, boots squishing. Clint Overhart said, "Will, where'd you come from?"

"Watch 'em. Kill 'em if they move again."

"You bet."

He was running toward Lucina. She had dropped her rifle and was running toward him. Tears were streaming down her face. Then she was in his arms, crying.

"I killed him, Will. I killed a man. I didn't want to. I killed him." Her shoulders shook as she sobbed.

Holding her tight, he tried to catch his breath, and finally managed, "It's all right, Lu. It's all right. You had to. He would've killed you."

Her voice was muffled against his shoulder, "I didn't want to. I shot him. I shot him down."

"It's all right. You did the right thing. If you hadn't fired some warning shots we'd all be dead. All of us."

"Oh, Will." She stepped back and wiped her eyes with the palms of her hands.

"Tell you what, Lu. Let's leave these packhorses at the wagon and go on to town. Somebody has to tell the sheriff about this. Let the laws clean up the bodies." He turned half around and yelled, "Anybody hurt?"

"Naw, Will," Clint Overhart answered. "We seen 'em comin'."

"But," the other cowboy said, "we didn't see 'em

176

cross the river. We'd of been in a trap if you hadn't come along."

"Do somethin' for me, will you?"

"Name it."

"Take these packhorses to the wagon and unsaddle 'em. Don't let anybody touch what's in the panniers."

"We'll do 'er."

"Come on, Lu, let's go to town. There's a big tub and plenty of hot water waitin' for you."

She carefully stepped around the dead man, but diverted her eyes from him as she walked back to the horses.

He had to go to the sheriff's house on the east side of town. It was a one story wood frame house with a corral and stable in back. The sheriff was a big man with a walrus mustache, and he was walking on crutches with his left leg wrapped in plaster when he answered the knock on his door. He swore when Will told him what had happened.

"I knew there was gonna be trouble as soon as I heard there was a bunch of Texas cattle out there. Why in holy hell can't you damn cowboys keep your goddamn noses clean?"

Will had been almost killed. So had Lucina and the cowboy crew. Will was getting damned tired of being blamed by the damned officers of the damned law. "Listen," he hissed through his teeth, "they started it. We didn't do anything but defend ourselves. They came at us and they came shootin'."

The sheriff's hard face turned harder. But Will wasn't through. "If your goddam law says we ain't got the right to defend ourselves then you know what you can do with your goddam law."

"Now you listen here, young feller . . ."

"Yeah?" Will stood with his feet apart and his hands on his hips. His eyes were locked onto the sheriff's eyes.

The sheriff had been standing up straight and tall on one foot, holding the crutches in front of him. Now he suddenly slumped and put a crutch under each armpit. When he spoke again, his voice was dry. "Goddam busted leg. Horse turned over on me. Helpless as a baby. All right, young feller, I'll get some men to go out to your camp and see for themselves. If it looks like it happened the way you said it did, then that, I hope, will be the goddam end of that."

Lucina was bathed and dressed in a clean cotton dress. Her short dark hair was brushed. She sat at a table in the hotel restaurant and waited for Will. He was going to the sheriff's house to report what had happened and then he was going to meet her here. She drank coffee and continually glanced at the door while she waited. When finally he did come in, he didn't stay.

"I've got to go back to the wagon with some of the sheriff's men," he said. "We have to get there before dark. There's no sign of Lucas yet. I'll come back to town as soon as I can."

Smiling to hide her disappointment, she said, "I understand, Will."

As she ate her roast beef and mashed potatoes, she was lonely, and she wondered how many dinners she would have to eat alone. And would she always sleep alone? Maybe being an entrepreneur and business-woman wasn't such a grand idea. No man would marry a woman who managed a business, who employed people, who . . . yes, bossed people, fired people. She ws destined to be lonely, a woman without a man.

Chewing slowly, she began thinking about following her mother's advice and giving up her plans for a business career. She hadn't reckoned with the loneliness. And she hadn't planned on having to shoot men. Could she be a ranch wife? She could if she wanted to. Will Porter was the kind of man she could live with.

Sleep with.

But he would be the lord and master and she would have to concern herself with nothing but wifely duties. Just like her mother.

Suddenly, she pushed her chair back, stood, and walked swiftly out of the restaurant. Other diners watched her go, curious. Her mind was full of confusion and indecision. And later, in her room alone, her mind was full of anger.

Dark clouds were gathering in the west when Lucina went out onto the plank walk next morning. Back there in the restaurant, where she had had breakfast, there was talk about the possibility of rain. The country was too dry. It needed rain. But rain wasn't the main topic of conversation. It was the shooting at the Texans' camp and the young woman who had shot and killed one of the men. Waitresses knew she was the one, and they had spread the word. She kept her head down and tried to ignore their curious glances and whispers. Outside, her footsteps turned toward the Rath and Wright general store. Inside, among the rows of clothing, groceries, and hand tools, she asked a clerk for either Mr. Wright or Mr. Rath. She was directed to a room in the back. The door was closed.

Here you go again, Lucina, she said to herself, trying to do business like a man. Gathering her resolve, she knocked, and entered when she was invited.

Robert M. Wright sat behind a huge desk piled with papers, bills of lading, lists of dry goods, lists of groceries, and money. Paper money. On top of a short stack of U.S. government greenbacks was a slip of paper with one name written on it: Vann.

"Mr. Rath?"

He stood, a thin man with a slightly receding chin and a thick mustache. "I am Robert Wright. Can I do something for you?"

Approaching the desk boldly, Lucina said, "Excuse me, Mr. Wright, I am Lucina Mays and, yes, I believe you can do something for me." She told him about the silver Mexican coins and how she had come by them.

He listened, eyes wide. "Your grandfather? He traded in Santa Fe?"

"Yes sir."

"Well, what do you know. Then you must be . . . yes, you are the young lady who was involved in a shooting yesterday at a cattle camp west of town." It was a statement, not a question, and Lucina only nodded. "Uhmm. Well, now. Why, yes, I make frequent trips to Wichita and Kansas City, and if you wish I will take the coins with me and convert them to U.S. currency."

"Fine. I will pay you a commission, of course."

"Oh, maybe a small commission. Since there's no bank in Dodge City I frequently act as banker for the local folk. That is, I handle their money for them. I don't lend money." He nodded at an iron safe as big as a kitchen stove against a wall behind the desk. "No money has been stolen from here as yet."

"The specie is in pack horse panniers now, Mr. Wright. Do you have a box to ship it in?"

"I'm sure we can find something."

"Fine. My friend and I will bring it here within the next few days." She started to leave, then turned back: "Uh, Mr. Wright, that name on the slip of paper there, I wonder if that by any chance is Mr. Jesse Vann, the town marshal?"

"Yes it is."

"Excuse my curiosity, sir, but does he own a business in Dodge City?"

"He manages a business for a group of investors."

Her eyebrows went up. "Oh really? Would it be, uh, excuse me again, Mr. Wright, but could you tell me what kind of business?"

Robert M. Wright smiled, but shook his head at the same time. "I'm sorry, Miss Mays, but I am not at liberty to discuss the affairs of private investors."

"Oh. Of course. Excuse me. I apologize for asking."

Outside the office, with the door closed behind her, she felt like the world's biggest fool. She should not have asked. It was very unprofessional. She should not have read any of the papers on Mr. Wright's desk. Lucina, she thought, you just make a jackass of yourself.

But she would have given a double eagle to know what kind of business Jesse Vann managed. And who the owners were.

Chapter Twenty-Two

When Will Porter rode down Trail Street, Lucina Mays waved and yelled to get his attention. "Yoohoo." And when he reined over, she said, "I'm happy to report, Will, that I do not have to go to Wichita to convert our specie."

"Our what? Oh, the Mexican coins. How are you gonna do it?"

"Mr. Wright at Rath and Wright will do it for us."

Dismounting, he said, "Well, that'll save you a trip. I don't reckon Lucas came in on the train last night?"

"No. I didn't see who came in, but I haven't seen him. Are you worried, Will?"

"Yeah. The railcars came in last night. They're sittin' out there on a side track. We can ship some of our cattle now. But I wish we had a buyer."

"Perhaps your uncle will arrive tonight."

"I hope so. Meantime, I'll go get that money and bring it to town."

"Shall I go with you?"

"No. Some of those gunsels are still alive and kickin' and they might be tickled to catch one or two of us alone."

"Perhaps you should wait for your uncle."

"No, I'll go get it."

He was back by noon, leading a packhorse loaded

with bulging panniers. "Boy," he said, "tyin' that stuff on one horse is like tyin' down two sacks of water. It keeps squirtin' around."

"Wait here, Will, and I'll go see Mr. Wright." When she came out of the store, she told Will to go around back, to a back door. There, Robert M. Wright met them and helped carry the money into his office.

"Do you want to count it?"

Lucina looked at Will for an answer. "Naw. I've asked, and you've got a reputation for bein' an honest man. Besides," he grinned, "it would take all day."

"Let's weigh it, then, and I'll give you a receipt. It's very possible that the bank will buy it by the pound, anyway."

"Whew," Lucina said, outside, "that's a load off my mind."

"And off our backs," Will said. "Do you think it's really worth twenty thousand dollars?"

"Who knows. The rate of exchange fluctuates. It could be worth much more."

"Well, I want to go count those cattle cars and try again to guess how many cattle they'll hold. As soon as Lucas gets back and the railroad sends an engine, we'll start loadin' cattle."

"I have nothing else to do. I'll go with you. That is, if you don't mind walking."

After a noon meal at the Dodge House, Will went back to the Porter camp and told the crew to start gathering the cattle. They would be shipping within a few days.

"Whooee," exclaimed Clint Overhart, "there's a faro dealer in Dodge City that owes me some chips. I cain't wait to git them cow brutes loaded and go collect."

"He'll collect your ass and all its fixtures, that's what he'll do," said China Eye. "You children never learn. You can't beat a man at his own game."

"Think there's gonna be anymore gunfire around here?"

"Them deputy shurff's or whatever they was picked up three dead men across the river. Them that survived won't be back."

"Naw. A burnt child stays away from fire."

"We shore smoked their asses."

"Will did. And that young woman. She's some gal. Purty too, when she takes off that sheepherder's hat."

With a crooked grin, Will said, "Clint, gather the herd about a mile east and hold 'em in a loose bunch where they'll be ready. I'm goin' back to town and hope Lucas comes in on the next train."

"We'll do 'er."

He stopped first at the livery, where he put up his horse, then walked to the Dodge House. Lucina met him in the lobby. From there they went to the depot. Old Number Forty-seven was on time, the stationmaster said. "She's a Mason Bogie Two-Six-Six, and she's pullin' twenty cattle cars empty, two boxcars, four flatbeds, a Pullman coach, and a caboose. That makes up the consist. She's a-rollin'."

Soon they heard the whistle and two minutes later saw the puffs of smoke. Ten minutes later Old Number Forty-seven rolled, rattled, hissed, and puffed into Dodge City. The engineer stopped her so the coach was in front of the depot platform. A porter was the first out. He placed an iron stool under the steps and watched the passengers dismount. Lucas Porter was behind a fat woman and two children.

"Howdy, Lucas. How's things?"

"Tolerable. Howdy, Miss Mays. Did you two find what you was lookin' for?"

Grinning, Will said, "That we did. We found more money than we could carry."

"Reckon a feller could get a cup of coffee over at the Dodge House? That stuff they give us on the train can bite back."

No more questions were asked until they were seated at a table with coffee mugs in front of them. Then Will

184

told his uncle about the cattle cars and asked about a buyer. Lucina kept quiet and looked from one man to the other.

"Found some buyers. I'm a little put out at the price they offered. One feller said his top price was two and a quarter cents a pound and another was so generous he offered two and a half. I figure they'll average about nine fifty a head, what would you guess?"

"That sounds about right."

"Another gent offered three cents a pound in Wichita. The railroad's gonna stick us a hundred and fifty per car to tote 'em to Wichita."

Will was trying to do some figuring in his head and wasn't making much progress. "Let's see, two and a half cents per pound times nine hundred and fifty pounds, that's, uh . . ."

Lucina answered, "Twenty-three dollars and seventy-five cents per animal."

Will stared at her in amazement. Lucas Porter said, "It took me a while to figure that out on a piece of paper. You've got a head for figures, Miss Mays."

"Call me Lu. My friends do. I've always been good at mathematics. You have two thousand eight hundred head?"

Will answered, "Minus one we gave to some Indians and one that China Eye butchered."

"Then at two and a half cents per pound you would total sixty-six thousand four hundred fifty-two dollars and fifty cents."

"Yeah?" Lucas Porter unfolded a sheet of paper he took from his hip pocket. "I've been figuring and refiguring all day and most of last night, and I get, uh, by George you're right. Ahmm, now then, at three cents per pound with us payin' the shippin' charges, it would come to, uh . . ." Unsure of himself, he watched Lucina's face.

"At three cents per pound you would get twenty-eight dollars and fifty cents per head for a total of seventy-nine thousand seven hundred and forty-three dollars."

"Ahmm, yeah, that's what I figured." Lucas Porter hastily refolded his sheet of paper and put it back in his pocket.

"Then," said Will, "would we realize more profit if we ship the cattle ourselves and pay the freight?"

"Not at all, Will." Lucina's face screwed up on concentration. "You estimated you'll need one hundred and forty cars. At one hundred and fifty dollars per car you would pay twenty-one thousand dollars shipping costs. If you sell them here at two and a half cents per pound and let the buyer pay the shipping costs, you would be far ahead—seven thousand seven hundred and nine dollars and fifty cents ahead."

Frowning and grinning at the same time, Lucas Porter said, "You ain't real. Are you sure about your figures."

"I'm sure."

"Then, heck, we'll sell 'em right here and let the buyer worry about payin' the railroad." He took a swallow of coffee. "I'd hoped for a little more per pound, but maybe I was hopin' for too much."

"Mr. Porter?" Lucina didn't know how to put the question without seeming officious, but she had to know. "Uh, it's none of my business and I know nothing about the cattle market, but did you happen to talk to a buyer named Goodwin?"

"Goodwin?"

"Yes. Of Goodwin & Sons Livestock Co. in Wichita."

"Oh, him. No, I tried to but he was in Illinois or someplace sellin' cattle to the corn farmers."

"Did anyone know when he'll be back?"

"S'posed to be back today. Why?"

"Well, please don't think I'm trying to tell you how to sell cattle, but it happens that I have met Mr. Goodwin and I mentioned a herd of Texas cattle near this city,

186

and he seemed to be interested."

"He was? Just my luck that I missed 'im."

"You could telegraph him."

Lucas Porter was looking into Lucina's eyes, looking intently. She flushed, "I'm sorry. It's none of my business. Please forgive me."

"Sure, I could send him a wire, but that's no way to do business. I like to meet the man I make a deal with."

"Oh, well, it was just an idea."

"You've met him, you say?"

"Yes sir."

"And you told him about our cattle?"

"Yes sir. I couldn't pass up the opportunity."

Lucas Porter turned his leathery face toward his nephew. "Where did you say you found this young lady?"

Chuckling, Will answered, "Out on the prairie. I told you I've never met anybody like her."

Turning back to Lucina, Lucas Porter said, "Do you reckon this gentleman would remember your palaver?"

"Yes sir, I believe he would."

"So if I send him a wire and mention your name he'll know what I'm talkin' about, wirin' him about?"

"Yes sir."

"I'll do it. Maybe you just showed me a faster way to do business."

At the depot, Lucas Porter took a lead pencil and a yellow form from the telegrapher and frowned at it a moment. "Derned if I know what to say. Miss Mays, Lu, you got any ideas?"

"Would you like me to write it?"

She wrote a lengthy message, but she believed it was worth what it cost. "Dear Mr. Goodwin," she began, "I am hoping you will remember our conversation of July 19 in the Wichita stockyards concerning 2800 Texas cattle now grazing near Dodge City. The cattle are ready for shipping and railcars are available. Please advise immediately if still interested. Direct your answer to Mr. Lucas Porter, owner of the cattle." She signed her name.

The telegrapher read it carefully and shook his head. "It's gonna take a while to punch this out."

"I apologize, but I don't think a briefer message would suffice."

"I'll pay whatever it costs," Lucas Porter said, pulling his leather wallet out of a shirt pocket.

It was dark as the two Porters left Lucina at her hotel lobby and walked in the moonlight to the livery barn to retrieve their horses. When they were three miles from town they found cattle in a loose bunch and grazing peacefully. Lucas Porter yelled to identify himself, and greeted his employees. "Any missin'?"

"Don't think so," Clint Overhart answered. "Haven't tallied 'em all yet, but we haven't seen any carcasses. When're we gonna load 'em?"

"Won't be more'n a few days now."

The news was encouraging next day. George Goodwin of Goodwin & Sons Livestock Co. had wired that he would arrive on the next westbound train. That pleased Lucas Porter. "I didn't wanta go back to Wichita, but I do want to see the man I do business with."

Will grinned. "Now, if he doesn't offer more money than the rest of 'em he'll have made a trip for nothin'."

"It shows he's interested, all right."

Will couldn't leave town without seeing Lucina, and he found her in the Dodge House lobby. "I'm just watching people go by," she said. "I'm a people watcher."

"So am I," Will said. "'Specially after bein' out in the tullies for a few months. I'm always tryin' to guess what other men do for a livin'."

"It takes all kinds to make the world go around. See that man over there, the one with the curly hair and the necktie? I don't know what he's selling, but I'll wager he just garnered a worthwhile order from Rath and Wright."

"What makes you think so?"

"The happy look on his face. No, it's a kind of self-satisfied look. I've seen the same expression on my brothers' faces when they made a big sale. And he's leaving on the next train east, I heard him say that. And by the way, Robert M. Wright left last night and he took our silver with him. We should get our spending money in a few days."

"I'm not gonna spend it 'till I get it. In fact, I'm not even gonna think about it yet. How about you?"

"I'm thinking. Oh yes, I'm thinking."

George Goodwin from Wichita was the first to step out of the Pullman car. Lucina pointed him out, but stayed back while Lucas Porter stepped up and introduced himself. She kept quiet until George Goodwin recognized her.

"Nice to see you again, Miss Mays. Glad you remembered me."

"It's nice to see you too, Mr. Goodwin."

The two Porters and Lucina accompanied the cattle buyer to the Dodge House and agreed to meet him there early next morning. They would bring an extra horse, a plumb gentle one, and the buyer would ride out to look at the cattle. He gave no hint at what he would offer.

Will promised to see Lucina again next day, but his "Adios" was interrupted by a well-dressed but travel-wrinkled man in a Prince Albert coat and derby hat.

"Excuse me, sir, but I'm told that you are Mr. Porter."

The older Porter answered, "I am Lucas Porter and this here is my nephew, Will Porter."

"Please excuse my appearance. I just arrived by rail. I've been told that you have a rather large herd of Texas cattle ready for market." His face was red and damp with perspiration from the August heat.

"Yes sir, we do. Twenty-eight hundred head."

"Mr. Porter, I represent the United Meat Produce Co. of Kansas City—my card." He handed Lucas Porter a small business card on which was printed Thom Jackson, United Meat Produce Co.

The older Porter read it.

"We are definitely looking for beef. I am prepared to offer you four cents per pound at Kansas City."

"But," Lucas Porter was puzzled, "I went to United Meat Produce Company's office and was told they was buyin' nothin' but corn-fed cattle."

"Unfortunately, I was away on a buying trip. I do a considerable amount of travel, buying beef and pork. It was not until I returned that I learned of your visit. Mr. Porter, I am the buyer for United."

As always when business was discussed, Lucina was listening. And thinking. Yes, there was a United packinghouse in Kansas City. But four cents per pound? She knew nothing about the price of beef on the hoof, buy why would this man offer so much more than anyone else? Never look a gift horse in the mouth, her oldest brother once said. But Grandfather Rathman had said, "If it sounds too good to be true, proceed as though you were walking into a den of snakes."

A warning was coiling itself in the pit of her stomach.

Chapter Twenty-Three

Lucas Porter's face screwed up on concentration as he tried to multiply in his mind. He turned to Lucina.

She said, "That would be thirty-eight dollars per head. Less shipping, it would be thirty dollars and fifty cents per head."

"Well now," Lucas Porter said. "Mr. Jackson, that's the best offer I've had so far. But there is another buyer interested, and I promised him I would let him see the cattle and consider his offer."

"You understand, Mr. Porter, that I have other livestock growers to talk to, and I must leave on the very next train. I am certain that no other buyer will offer you as much as United. If you wish we can draw up the sale papers immediately, I can write you a bank draft or pay you some cash, whichever you prefer, and I can be on my way."

"You're ready to pay right now? In cash?"

"Yes sir."

"We-e-el." Lucas Porter turned to Lucina.

"The total would be one hundred six thousand, three hundred and twenty four dollars."

"And you're ready, Mr. Jackson, to hand over that much cash?"

"Well, uh, naturally I don't carry that much on my person, what with all the lawlessness in the west. But I can pay you, let's see, thirty thousand dollars now and the balance on delivery."

"Cash money?"

"Yes, sir. We can make out the papers now, you can bill the cattle to me at the Kansas City stockyards, and I will be there to pay the balance when you arrive with them."

Turning to Will, Lucas Porter said, "Whatta you think, Will?"

"Sounds good. I'll go to Kansas City any time for that much money."

"Then it's agreed? I can leave on the next eastbound, and expect the cattle in the very near future."

"Hmm." Lucas Porter studied his boots. "I hate to take your offer without findin' out what George Goodwin will offer. Hmm. Would you wait a minute while I run upstairs and ask 'im. I have to give him a fair chance."

"Of course. But hurry please."

Lucas Porter was gone only ten minutes. While he was gone Lucina was thinking. That warning in the pit of her stomach grew. When the older Porter came back down the stairs he wore a frown. "George Goodwin said he wouldn't no way pay more'n two and three-quarters cents per pound on the prairie. That's a lot less. He's plenty put out by your offer, Mr. Jackson."

"Well, they are your cattle and you can sell to whomever you wish. However, I must have your decision within the hour."

"Whatta you think, Will?"

"We're in the cattle business. We have to take the best offer. Mr. Goodwin ought to understand that. Uh, Lucina, what do you think?"

"Mr. Porter. Will. May I talk with you for a moment? Privately?"

"Why shore, Miss Mays. You've been a big help, and we'll listen to anything you've got to say."

They went to a far corner of the lobby and stood

192

close together. "Listen, Mr. Porter, Will, again I apologize. I never intended, when I came to Dodge City, to be in the middle of negotiations over cattle. But two things worry me. One, he is not ready to pay you the full price now. Two, he said you should bill the cattle to him." She paused to see if they were thinking the same thing she was thinking.

A small strangling sound came from Will. Lucas Porter's eyebrows went up so high they disappeared under his hat.

Lucina continued, "Now, if he claimed the cattle in Kansas City and refused to pay the balance, you could probably go to court and get one or the other. But the wheels of justice move slowly. Litigation takes time and it costs money. In the meantime—again, I know nothing about livestock—but you would have to feed the cattle and pay for the feed. To save you all that time and money, he—I'm only surmising here—he would talk you into settling out of court for considerably less than he promised."

"Oh-o-o," Will groaned. His uncle said nothing. His jaws were clamped tight. Turning on his heels he marched straight to where Thomas Jackson was waiting. Will and Lucina followed.

"Mr. Jackson, we've talked it over and we decided that you either pay the full price for our cattle here and now or we bill the cattle to ourselves. Is that agreeable?"

"Well, uh, ahem, Mr. Porter, as I said, I don't carry that much cash on my person. I can write you a draft on the Kansas City National Bank, a draft that is redeemable in any national bank in the nation."

Lucas Porter turned to Lucina. She only closed her eyes for a second.

Will Porter said, "No."

"What? Mr. Porter, do I understand that your nephew makes decisions of such importance?"

"He just did."

"Well, I never . . . and do you get your business advice from this young, uh . . ."

"Don't you say one insultin' word about her," Lucas Porter warned. "Not unless you wanta land on your backside."

After Thomas Jackson left, Lucas Porter looked down at his scuffed boots and shook his head. "I oughta be kicked all the way back to Texas. I'm so dumb I—"

Lucina cut in, "You're not so dumb, Mr. Porter. I have a feeling that in Texas you men do business with a promise and a handshake. I was reared in a family of businessmen, and in Kansas City, well, as my Grandfather Mays once said, "Tell them to put up the money or shut up.""

Still shaking his head, the older Porter said, "Just the same, if it hadn't been for you, uh . . ."

"Don't give me any credit. For all I know his offer was legitimate, and I just lost you a lot of money."

"Naw. Now, I'm no businessman, but I know somethin' about men, and that feller . . . the way he stormed out of here, he had a scheme and it just got snuffed out."

Will shuffled his feet and said, "If there's anything we can do for you, Lu, holler."

"You already have. You know you have. Now," she rubbed her hands together, "I can't wait to find out what Mr. George Goodwin will offer." Then she added, "Oh, excuse me again. The way I talked you'd think they were my cattle."

"You don't need to apologize," Lucas Porter said. "You don't ever need to apologize to the Porter clan."

They found George Goodwin at breakfast in the hotel restaurant, and they shared a table and a pot of coffee with him. Lucina came in before they were finished, and she too was invited to sit at the table. Though she was bursting with curiosity about any business that had been discussed, all she said was,

194

"Good morning."

Finally, Will said, "Care to ride out with us, Lu? The herd is only two or three miles from town."

She wanted to go, wanted to very much, but she would be out of place. "Oh, uh, thank you, but no. I know nothing about cattle, and you men will have business to discuss."

After they left, she was restless and lonely. She realized that she could not loaf around Dodge City much longer. She was going to have to do something to occupy her time—and soon. She went out onto the plank walk and watched the traffic go by. Traffic was light. No wagons loaded with buffalo hides had been seen for several days. No buffalo hunters had been seen since the day Will Porter was jailed. Inside Rath and Wright, customers were few. Lucina inspected the goods, smiled pleasantly at the clerk, and went back outside. Down the street a block, in the Moorehouse Mercantile, she found only two women customers, and she noticed that the store stocked almost exactly the same products as Rath and Wright: boots that laced up and jackboots that could be pulled on, heavy denim pants, wool shirts, the kind that would shrink if washed, socks, men's underwear.

Feeling eyes on her back, Lucina turned and saw the two women customers watching her curiously as she inspected the men's clothing. She smiled and nodded. "Good morning. Is it ever going to rain?" Out West, she had learned, the weather was a favorite topic of conversation.

The morning sun was already burning down, and heat waves shimmered out over the prairie when Lucina left the store. Would Will find her and inform her of what transpired between the Porters and the cattle buyer? Of course he would. He knew she was interested.

*   *   *

195

George Goodwin took his time riding through the cattle. He knew how to sit a saddle, but he was not as comfortable on a horse as the cattlemen. Finally, he reined over to the Porters. "Like I said last night, my top price for beef on the prairie is two and three-quarters per pound. How much do you figure they'll weigh on the average?"

"Nine fifty," Lucas Porter answered.

"Hmm. I've seen a lot of cattle weighed, and I would guess nine hundred. Well, maybe, to give you the benefit of the doubt, nine twenty-five."

Lucas Porter glanced at Will. Will said, "Nope. Some of 'em'll weigh considerably less, but some will weigh more. Nine fifty is givin' you the benefit of the doubt."

The buyer squinted at Will a moment, then at Lucas, then back at Will. His borrowed horse shuffled its feet impatiently. "I recognize the fact that you were offered more by a buyer from United. But somehow you didn't take his offer." He squinted at the horizon a moment, then, "All right, nine fifty."

"At two and three-quarter cents per pound, you've bought a herd of cattle."

"Well now, all I said was two and three-quarter cents was my top price. That's for a beefier breed of cattle."

"These beefs will taste just as good as any breed," Lucas Porter said. "The only difference is they won't weigh as much."

"And," Will added, "you're buyin' by the pound."

"Well now." George Goodwin dismounted and squatted on his heels, cowboy fashion. The Porters did the same, facing him. "Suppose I give you my top price, will you and your cowboys load them in the cattle cars for me?"

"Yup. We'll do that."

"Providin'," Will said, "that you can arrange for the cars sometime in the near future."

"Oh, I believe I can do that. I do a lot of business with

the railroads."

"We're talkin' about cash money?"

"Yes, if you insist. Of course I'd rather pay by bank draft, but if you insist, I'll pay cash." George Goodwin stood and stretched his legs. "As soon as the cattle are counted and loaded."

The Porters stood too and shook hands with the buyer. "All right," Lucas Porter said, "let's go to the telegraph desk and find out how soon the railroad can get an engine out here. We're ready to ship."

They were a mile from town when they saw a horseman coming toward them. The silver star pinned on his shirt glinted in the sun, and they knew immediately who he was. "Wonder what that yahoo wants," Will muttered.

"We're out of his jurisdiction," the older Porter said, "but I got a hunch he ain't packin' good news."

They all reined up when they met. No one spoke for a moment. The marshal's cold stare was met by cold stares from the Porters. George Goodwin looked from one man to another, puzzled. Finally, the marshal said:

"I want them cattle off my land right now."

Will had a strong urge to say something provocative, but he let his uncle speak first. "Your land? This is free range."

"Not anymore it ain't. I just claimed a hundred and sixty acres of it."

"The hell you beller." Lucas Porter squinted at the marshal from under his hat brim. "What's a hundred and sixty acres more or less? We'll move 'em."

"Across the river."

"Huh? Naw, we ain't crossin' the river. Hell, we'd have to cross it twice, now and again when we ship. Naw, if you're homesteadin' a hundred and sixty acres, we'll move 'em north, but not south."

Nodding toward the north, the marshal said, "That land's been claimed too. That means you move south."

"The hell you beller. Will, whatta you say?"

Will sat his saddle solidly, hat pulled low, ready for anything. "Well," he drawled, speaking slower than usual, "I don't know nothin' about the homestead laws, but I do believe you have to prove up on your claim. Now"—he glanced back the way they had come—"I didn't see a shack, a plow or anything. Tell you the truth, I don't think you've got a right to order us to move."

"That's the way I see it too, marshal," the older Porter said. "Seems like you're goin' out of your way to make it hard on us, and I can't help wonderin' why."

"I told him," the marshal nodded at Will, "that I wouldn't allow no Texas cattle and no Texas cowboys around here."

For a long moment it was a stare-down. Then, without taking his eyes away from the marshal's eyes, Lucas Porter said, "Mr. Goodwin, why don't you go on back to town. We'll get this settled and we'll meet you at the hotel."

"Ahem, yes, this is not my affair. Yes, I'll do that." George Goodwin kicked the horse's sides with his shoe heels and rode away at a trot.

"Tie that horse to the hitchrail in front of the hotel," Lucas Porter said to Goodwin's back. "He'll stay put . . . Now then, marshal, we're goin' to ship these beefs out of here in a few days, and that'll be the end of that. There's been some men killed already. We don't want no more trouble."

"Is that so. You Texans are trouble. Everywhere you go there's trouble. Well, I, by God, ain't gonna allow it around here. Take my word for it, some of you're gonna gt killed." The marshal pulled his horse around so hard the animal had to open its mouth and throw its nose up to relieve the pressure.

Chapter Twenty-Four

An engine and twenty more cattle cars would be on their way next day just ahead of the regular westbound, George Goodwin reported. The engine could pull twenty-two loaded cars. The news was good and bad. The cattlemen were happy to get started shipping cattle, but they realized it was going to take more than a few days to get the whole herd on its way. Will had hunted up Lucina and she was listening to the conversation.

"Twenty-two cars times twenty head per car is . . ." Will looked at Lucina.

"Four hundred, forty-four head per trainload. That's, uh, six trainloads. That is, if you can crowd three more head in. Boy, that's a lot of cattle."

"If they keep the engines and empty cars comin' we'll be done in a week."

"I believe they will," the cattle buyer said.

Next day the work began. The cowboys cut out four hundred and forty head, and had them in the pens ready for loading. It took two hours to crowd the cattle up a loading chute and into the cars. Will had missed his guess by one. The cars could have held twenty-one head.

"They'll lose weight en route," the cattle buyer mused, "but we'll feed and water them when they arrive, and they'll soon be healthy again."

The big black steam engine with a diamond smokestack and six big drive wheels puffed, belched fire, hissed steam, spun its wheels, and got the string of cars rolling.

"They'll feed a lot of easterners," Lucas Porter allowed.

"Yeah," his nephew said. But Will was feeling a little sad. He had lived with those animals for a long time and now they were headed for their deaths. It was not a happy thought. Aw, hell, he muttered under his breath, I didn't make the world. I'm just tryin' to live in it.

The Double O wagon was spotted just west of town. The older Porter talked the cowboys into staying out of town until the last steer was loaded. There was no disagreement. The men knew when they were hired on that the boss didn't have to pay them until the work was done. China Eye was more than happy to wait. He said he planned to get a haircut, buy some new clothes, and drive the wagon back to Texas.

The cattle shipping resumed next day. And the next.

At the end of the fourth day of loading cattle, Will and his uncle found themselves alone at the wagon while the crew was gathering cattle in the dusk. "Whatta you think, Will?" Lucas Porter asked.

"About what?"

"You know what."

"I don't know what to think. And I sure as hell don't know what to do about it."

"We've got enough men and guns here to take over the damn town if we have to."

"But you don't wanta do that."

"No, I don't, and won't. But that marshal worries me. That's why I'm keeping the crew out of town. He'd have half of 'em locked up in his jail by now."

"They're good men. I haven't heard one gripe."

"Just the same, I can't help wonderin' when the hammer's gonna fall."

The hammer fell the next day.

George Goodwin didn't show up to count the cattle as they were loaded. He didn't show up until the last car door was slammed shut and locked. When he did he was bareheaded—except for a big white bandage on top of his head.

His eyes were liquid and his round face seemed to have shrunk, with the cheeks drawn in and the heavy jowls running down into his shirt collar.

"Uh-oh," Will muttered.

"That's bad news if I ever saw it," Lucas Porter said.

They leaned against the side of an empty pen and waited for him to come close enough to talk. The cattle buyer was shaking his head before he got to them.

"I'm real sorry, gentlemen. I no longer have the money to pay you."

They waited for him to explain.

"I was robbed last night."

The three of them sat on the end of the loading chute and talked. It was simple robbery. Word had gotten around that George Goodwin was in town to buy that herd of cattle west of town, and he no doubt had the cash to pay. There was a knock on his hotel room door at night. When he asked who was there, someone answered, "Lucas Porter." He opened the door and was shoved back into the room and hit on the head.

There was only one man, and the cattle buyer described him to the sheriff and marshal right down to the jackboots. He was average. Nothing to make it easy for a lawman to recognize him. The sheriff had hobbled around on his crutches and sent telegraphs to sheriffs in all directions asking them to be on the lookout. The marshal had asked around town, and no one remembered seeing the man.

Lucas Porter had picked up a stick and was whittling on it with a pocketknife while he listened. 'That could change our plans," he said.

"Can you write us a bank draft?" Will asked.

201

"I don't think so. I'm not sure my company can stand the loss. There was seventy-five thousand dollars in that bag."

"Too bad there ain't a national bank around here so you wouldn't have to pack that much around."

"Doing business in the West has its hazards." George Goodwin seemed on the verge of tears. "I could have made a profit on these cattle. The railroad was giving me a special rate because I do so much stock shipping. And we have our own stockyards and feed." He rubbed a hand over his face. "I could have made a good profit."

"Did he hurt you bad?"

"I was out cold for at least an hour. That excuse for a doctor took thirteen stitches in the top of my head."

Squinting at the horizon, Lucas Porter said, "We've been billing these cattle to the Goodwin & Sons Livestock Company. We'll bill the rest of 'em that way if you think you can pay for 'em."

"I apologize. I can't promise. I'm not sure we can raise that much."

"Looks like we'll have to bill 'em to ourselves and go to Wichita and find another buyer."

"I apologize, gentlemen."

"No apologies needed. You're not at fault. I hope you get lucky and get your money back."

Will stood and looked at the sky. There were several hours of daylight left. "I'm goin' for a ride."

"Got an idea, Will?"

"I don't know. We'll see." He stomped over to a half dozen cowboys who were squatting in the shade of a railcar. "Clint, get on your horse."

They rode around the west end of Dodge City and circled to the north side before Will spoke again. "Clint, you're a good tracker. Better than I am. Look for one horse goin' at a lope."

"I already seen it."

"Which direction was he goin'?"

"Straight north. He was foggin' it."

"Do you know when?"

The cowboy dismounted, squatted on his boot heels, and studied the tracks. "After dark and before sunup. The ground was cool then."

"One horse?"

"Yup. Nope. Another'n here. Now there's two of 'em. One of 'em was waitin' right here."

"Keep your eyes on 'em. Let's lope."

They rode at a slow gallop until Clint Overhart reined up. "One came back. Headed for town."

"Just one came back?"

"Yup. It was the one that was waitin'."

"You sure? How can you tell, Clint?"

"Both horses was barefooted, but that'n that came back would take a One. The other'n is a Ought." The cowboy shot a curious glance at Will. "You gonna tell me what we're lookin' for?"

"Money," Will said, and slapped spurs to his horse.

As long as he could see the tracks, Will led the way, but at one place where the grass was thick he had to slow down and let Clint Overhart lead. Clint stopped, got down, and studied the ground. But when he mounted again, he pointed to the north-northwest. "Headed straight for someplace. They knew where they were goin'."

They scattered a small bunch of red Durham cattle and kept riding at a slow gallop. Soon they saw the sod shack that they'd seen before, but the tracks went on past it. A half mile farther they came to the ravine and the dugout shelter. Clint pulled up. "They stopped here, tied their horses to that bush, and went inside." The cowboy studied the ground another moment, and added, "Mounted up again and one headed on north at a lope whilst the other'n went back."

"He went right straight to that big house up there, didn't he?" Will said. "I had a suspicion he would."

"What's goin' on, Will?"

Without answering, Will got down and ducked his

203

head as he entered the dugout. It was empty. Clint followed him. "Lookin' for money, you said?"

"Yeah."

"Well, I'll bet I'm standin' on it."

"Huh? Well, I'll be damned. I don't see no shovel so it can't be buried deep."

"Here's the stick he used to dig a hole. He tried to brush out the sign, but hell, any fool could see where he'd patted the dirt down with his hands. Over here's some burnt matches. One of 'em struck matches so the other could see what he was doin'."

The heavy canvas bag was buried only four inches below the surface. Will pulled it out, opened it and whistled. "Look at this. Gaw-ed damn."

"Whew. When you said money, Will, you meant money. How much you reckon's there."

"S'posed to be seventy-five thousand. Look, all fifty-dollar bills. No, here's some hundreds."

"Will Porter, I'm gonna take a look outside to make sure there ain't nobody around, and then I hope you're gonna tell me what's goin' on."

Grinning widely, Will said, "Sure. It's a story you can tell to your grandkids. If you ever have any."

It turned dark before they got back to town, and that disappointed Will. "I'd give my interest in hell to find out where that other horse went."

"Back to town, that's for shore."

"Yeah, but where in town?"

"I can track 'em in the mornin', but when they get to town they'll be mixed with a lot of other tracks."

"The trail will be cold then, but damn, I'd sure like to know who was ridin' that horse."

At the edge of Dodge City, the two men split up. Clint went to the Double O wagon to tell Lucas Porter about the found money, and Will went to the Dodge House. He carried the heavy canvas bag under his left arm as he went up the stairs and knocked on George Goodwin's door.

"It's Will Porter, Mr. Goodwin. It really is."

The door opened a careful crack and then wider. The cattle buyer was in a long white nightgown, and he explained that he was about to retire for the night. Will held the bag behind his back when he entered. "What was your money in, Mr. Goodwin?"

Eyeing the young man curiously, George Goodwin said, "Why, I carried it in a leather grip. This one here." He nodded at a satchel on the floor beside a bigger suitcase.

"That's all?"

"Well, it was in a canvas bag. I put the bag in the satchel, hoping no one would suspect that I was carrying money."

Will handed him the bag. "Is this it?"

It took a while for the shock and surprise to wear off, and then George Goodwin was so thankful he was speechless. Will gave full credit to the cowboy named Clint Overhart. "He can track a crow in flight," Will said. And then he excused himself and said good night.

In the corridor, he looked in the direction of Lucina's room and considered knocking on her door. She would be interested in hearing about everything, and besides, he wanted to visit with her. After all, she did invite him to her room when she had something to tell him. Now he had something to tell her. Why not? He marched to her door. Floorboards creaked under his boots. His spurs chinged.

Now. She's probably in bed. Or at least in her bedclothes. She wouldn't appreciate a visitor at bedtime.

But dammit, he wanted to talk to her, and tomorrow he'd be too busy loading cattle. What to do?

Bending over, he studied the bottom edge of her door. Was there a light on the other side? Yeah. At least she wasn't in bed. All right. Go ahead. Knock. He knocked.

"Who's there?"

"Will Porter."

"Will who?"

Huh? She knew who. No, she was just being careful. After what had happened the night before she wasn't going to open the door to just anybody. "It's Will Porter, Lu. I'd like to talk to you."

"One minute, Will."

When she opened the door she was wearing a rose-colored robe that covered her from throat to ankles. It was belted tightly, and it showed the curves in her body. "Will, did something happen?"

"Yeah. Yes. Excuse me for botherin' you. There's somethin' I'd like to talk to you about."

She stepped back. "Come in."

Again he stood until she invited him to sit on the one chair. Again he sat on the edge of it and held his hat in his hands. She sat on the bed with her knees together and her hands between her knees. He said, "You heard about George Goodwin gettin' robbed?"

"Yes. Terrible. The poor man."

"We got the money back."

She jerked up straight. "What?"

For the second time that night he told about it, giving full credit to Clint Overhart. "What I wanted to talk to you about, Lu, is you've been in Dodge City for a few months now, and you've heard about that Durham ranch north of town?"

"Yes. It's kind of mysterious. Seems it is owned by an eastern financier. A nameless, faceless individual."

"I've got a hunch the marshal's connected with it, somehow."

"Oh, really?"

"Yeah, and I've got another hunch. I can't prove it and maybe I never will, but . . ."

"What, Will?"

"I've got a hunch the marshal helped rob George Goodwin."

Chapter Twenty-Five

Lucina gasped, "You don't . . . really!"

"Look at it this way: A man robbed George Goodwin. Then the robber met another man just outside of town. The two went north to that dugout where they hid the money, and the second man came back to town. Don't you see? Somebody here in town was in on the whole thing, and it was somebody who'd be easy to recognize.

The pair of 'em planned to divvy the money later. They would have done it last night but it was too dark to count money. In the daytime, somebody from the Durham ranch might see 'em. So they're goin' back tonight with a lantern. They're gonna be disappointed."

"And very, very angry."

Will grinned. "Won't they? Anyhow, the marshal wanted us out of this part of the country. He says Texas cowboys are nothin' but trouble. But it sounds phony, doesn't it? Whoever owns the Durham ranch wants us out for a couple of reasons: tick fever and because he wants to take over the whole territory. That, I can understand. I can even understand why he'd hire a bunch of gun hands to try and shoot us out. What I can't understand is why the marshal is so damned determined to get rid of us."

"Unless," Lucina added thoughtfully, "he has an

interest in that ranch."

"Yeah. He goes up there every now and then. The livery owner—Easton—told me once the marshal goes up north and practices with his six-shooter every day and sometimes he's gone most of the day. I'll bet he goes up to that ranch."

"And the robber went to the ranch while his cohort came back to town."

"I got a look at the marshal's horse once, but I didn't pay much attention to him. I'd like to get another look at 'im."

"Why?"

"The horse that went to the dugout and back last night would take ones, and I'd like to—"

She interrupted, "Ones?"

"Shoes. Horseshoes. The horse was barefooted like most prairie horses are, but his hooves are the size that would take a number one shoe."

"Oh. Is that uncommon?"

Shaking his head, Will answered, "Naw, not too uncommon. Most horses around here would take oughts or double oughts, but ones ain't too uncommon."

"But it would be another clue."

"Yup. If I remember right the marshal's horse is a little bigger than most."

They were silent, deep in thought; then, "You're smarter than me, Lu, what do you think of all this?"

"I'm not smarter than you. My mind runs in a different track, is all. I think we should get a look at the marshal's horse, and there's something else, now that I'm thinking about it."

He kept quiet, waiting for her to go on.

"A sum of money was sent to Jesse Vann—the marshal—from somewhere back east. I saw it in Mr. Wright's office at the mercantile. Could it be . . . could that money have been sent to pay wages at the ranch? If so, that would mean the marshal is managing the ranch."

"It could be. In fact, I'd bet on it."

"Hmm. Interesting. Very, very interesting. Are you going to tell the sheriff about the money?"

"I reckon I'll have to. If he didn't have a busted leg I'd let him come to me, but as it is, I'll go see 'im first thing in the mornin'."

"I think that would be wise. He might even find out who all is involved."

A wry grin turned up one corner of Will's mouth. "He might. Meantime, I've got to get back to the wagon. Lucas probably thinks I got throwed in jail again." He stood, went to the door.

"Be careful, Will. Jesse Vann is a very dangerous man."

The Atichison, Topeka & Santa Fe kept one steam engine busy running back and forth between Dodge City and Wichita, pulling loaded cars east and empty cars west. In a week the job was done. Toward the end of the week Robert M. Wright returned from Kansas City with U.S. paper currency for Lucina Mays. She had to go to his office to collect it, and he had to take it out of his safe. When he opened the safe he had to separate her money from another bundle of currency which was wrapped with a paper band. Printed on the band were the words: FIRST NATIONAL BANK OF KANSAS CITY.

Lucina was familiar with that bank. Her grandfather Rathman was on its board of directors. She carried the money to her room in a paper wrapper and waited for Will Porter to come calling. But her head was full of ideas and she couldn't sit still. After locking the door behind her, she went first to the railroad depot and sent a wire to her grandfather, then she went two blocks down the plank walk to the Moorehouse Mercantile. Inside, she asked a clerk for Mr. Moorhouse.

"I am Mr. Moorhouse," the clerk said.

"Mr. Moorhouse, I am Lucina Mays. If you have a moment to spare, I would like to speak to you about a business matter."

"As you can see, Miss Mays, I have no customers and plenty of time. What sort of business matter?"

At the railroad pens, Will, his uncle, and George Goodwin squatted on the ground with a well-worn saddle blanket between them. The cattle buyer opened his leather satchel and counted out exactly seventy-three thousand ninety-seven dollars and seventy-five cents. He laid each bill and silver coin on the saddle blanket one at a time. Will held his hand on the pile of bills to keep the prairie wind from blowing them away.

"I want to give you a reward for finding my money after it was stolen."

"You don't owe me anything, but I can't speak for Clint."

"Would you give him this?" George Goodwin handed over two fifty-dollar bills. "Were it not for him, we, none of us, would be sitting here counting this money."

"You're right. I had a hunch about it, but I'm not the tracker he is and I couldn't have tracked it down. He'll be mighty pleased."

"I'll be traveling in the way car," George Goodwin said. "I'll get to Wichita tomorrow morning." He stood. The Porters stood. "Gentlemen, it was a pleasure doing business with you. If you happen to bring more cattle to Kansas, wire me."

Lucas Porter said, "We surely will, Mr. Goodwin. Pleasure doin' business with you." He folded his stack of bills and stuffed them into his pants pockets.

It was done.

At the cattle camp, Lucas Porter paid off the crew. "You boys are welcome to ride my horses back to the ranch," he said. "Or you can stay or head for some big

210

city or whatever you want. Will and me, we can drive the remuda back by ourselves if we have to."

"I ain't takin' no stage to Texas," Clint Overhart allowed. "I'll go back with you. But first I got to spend some of this U.S. government greenback money."

"Me too," said another cowboy. "I'll be here and ready to go in the mornin'."

"If I didn't need a haircut and some new rags," said China Eye, "I wouldn't even go to town. You boys won't recognize me when I get back."

"I hope you get a new pair of britches, China Eye. Them you're wearin' killed the grass when you dropped 'em on the ground last night."

"If you think his britches're rank you oughta smell his blankets. Even the bedbugs cain't stand 'em."

"He must of let a million farts in them blankets."

"He never had to worry about no rattlers gettin' in bed with 'im."

"Say, China Eye, if we buy you some new blankets, will you burn them old ones?"

"My garsh." A cowboy looked stricken. "We cain't do that. If the smoke should happen to drift over Dodge City it'd kill ever' man, woman and child."

"If we throw 'em in the river they'll pizen the water."

"There ain't but one thing to do, boys." Clint Overhart drew his six-gun, cocked the hammer back, and aimed it at China Eye's rolled-up bed. "Kill 'em, then get back to Texas before the dead rot sets in."

Amid whoops, hollers, and guffaws, a dozen .44 cartridges exploded, and the cook's bed was filled with bullet holes.

China Eye leaned against a wagon wheel and watched quietly until the gunsmoke cleared. Then he spoke calmly, seriously, "Fellers, did you ever see a man die of toe-main poison? Well, I'll tell you what happens. First his guts turn wrong side out, and then his face turns black and then his tongue sticks out so far you could hang a horse collar on it, and when he tries to talk all he can do is choke and throw up, and then his head swells up so big it pops open like a rotten watermelon."

His blank eye was fixed on them. He had their attention.

"And that ain't all. He pees down his pants leg and shits his drawers and his feet get to runnin', and they ain't got no brain to tell 'em which way to go so they run around in crazy circles with his bloody remains floppin' around on top of 'em. And nobody wants to ketch 'im and put 'im out of his misery 'cause nobody can stand the putrefyin' sight of 'im."

The cowboy cook paused. No one else spoke. "Now then, I want two dollars a head from you gents. No, make that three dollars a head. I know how to make toe-main poison."

Thirty minutes later the cowboy crew was saddled and heading for Trail Street, whooping and hollering. Lucina heard them coming. Nearly everyone in town heard them coming. The bartenders reached under the bars for the rottenest whiskey, the card sharps shuffled the cards and exercised their dealing fingers, and the prostitutes began putting on their best clothes and painting their faces.

Marshal Jesse Vann heard them coming, and practiced his fast draw before going out onto the street.

Chapter Twenty-Six

Will and Lucas Porter divided the money and put it in pockets attached to two leather belts. They buckled the belts around their waists. Cattlemen had been robbed after selling herds of cattle. It was another danger they had to face.

"I didn't wanta say anything, but I hope the boys ride back with us," Lucas Porter said. "Nobody's gonna try to rob the whole crew."

"I think I'll leave mine in the safe at Rath and Wright 'till we get started," Will allowed. "Lu said they'll keep folks' money for 'em."

"Sounds like a good idee. Take mine too, all but a few bucks."

Lucina had met Robert M. Wright, had done business with him, so Will found her in her room and asked her to accompany him to the mercantile. It was another excuse to see her. She was more than willing, but first she had other things to talk about.

"Here," she said when Will took his usual seat on the edge of the chair in her room. She handed him a packet of greenbacks. "There's twelve thousand dollars."

"Huh? That much?"

"Yep. Those Mexican coins were worth twenty-four thousand three hundred dollars. I gave Mr. Wright three hundred for handling the transaction for us. My grandfather's trade goods, wagons and mules weren't worth as much as twenty-eight hundred cattle, but I'm sure he made a good profit."

"Those cattle weren't all profit, you know. Lucas borrowed from a bank in San Antonio, and raisin' that much beef costs money too. But, listen, I agreed to a quarter of what your granddad's treasure was worth. You gave me too much."

"I know what we agreed on, but I want you to have half."

"Oh no." He counted out six thousand dollars and, when she refused to take it, laid it on the bed beside her. "A deal is a deal."

"Will Porter, you are giving up six thousand dollars. Do you know what you can do with six thousand dollars?"

"Yeah, but I'll bet you can find some use for it too."

"Well, as a matter of fact." She stood. Her blue cotton dress reached from her throat to her shoes. "You are looking at the new owner of Mays General Store, formerly Moorhouse Mercantile."

"You don't say? You're gonna run a store?"

"Yep. I own it, lock, stock and barrel. You can help."

"Me? Help run a store?"

"Not run it. Listen, Will, as I said before, Dodge City is going to be crowded with Texas cowboys next spring. When word gets arond that you and your uncle sold a large herd here, most of the cattle drovers who have been going to Wichita will be coming here. I intend to cater to the cowboys in the spring, summer and fall, and to the local folks in the winter. You can advise me on what kind of merchandise to stock for cowboys. With your help, I'll have exactly what they want to buy. Will you do that?"

"Sure. Do you wanta make a list?"

"I've got catalogs from the wholesalers. It won't take much of your time to show me what to order. But first, there's something else I have to tell you. Look at this."

She took a yellow sheet of paper from a dresser drawer and handed it to him. It was from William L. Rathman, First National Bank of Kansas City. It read:

"Re your query Jesse Van borrowed from First National to start a ranch with Durham cattle in Western Kansas stop. Bank recently advanced funds to expand holdings stop. Expect next payment on note in October stop."

Will looked up at Lucina, puzzled. "What . . . does this mean what it looks like?"

"Yep. That Durham ranch is not financed by anyone but Jesse Vann and the First National Bank of Kansas City. My grandfather Rathman is on the bank's board of directors. I wired him a query as a prospective store owner who could be asked to advance credit to one Jesse Vann. That is a perfectly legitimate query."

"Well I'll be damned—darned. Wonder why he kept it a secret?" The puzzled frown on Will's face deepened. Then he brightened and said, "Oh, I see."

"You do?"

"Sure. It was Easton at the livery barn who suspicioned it first. He said somebody from back east was payin' those gunsels at the Durham ranch to homestead land and deed it over to him. It's a cheap way of buyin' land."

"And it's illegal. That's why he's so secretive."

"Yup. He made folks believe an easterner was bankrollin' the ranch. And when the homestead are proved up on he can say he bought 'em fair and square."

"That is why he doesn't want any Texas cattle around here. He's afraid of Texas fever, and he wants more of the land, the land Texas cattle will graze on every summer. It explains why he tried to discourage you from bringing your herd here and why he tried to get you to keep them across the river."

"Right. It figures."

"We can't let him get away with it. I'll go to the

sheriff. If that doesn't work, I'll go to the U.S land agent. Offhand I don't know where the nearest land agent is, but I'll find one."

"It might be hard to prove. The men he hired are still there at his ranch, the ones that didn't get killed in a gunfight with our crew. They can say they're workin' at the ranch part of the time to make livin' expenses while they prove up on their claims."

"Uh-huh. When they hear that the U.S. government is interested, they'll head for their dugouts or sod shacks and pretend they're living on their claims. Proving otherwise won't be easy, but I'll have to try."

"I'll go to the sheriff's house with you."

Robert M. Wright gave them a receipt and locked their money in his heavy safe. They walked to the sheriff's house. The sheriff was in a grumpy mood, still hobbling on crutches. But he invited them in and sat them on a velvet sofa while he sat on a wooden chair with his plaster-wrapped leg across the seat of another chair. His wife was at the mercantile, he said. Lucina didn't mention that she now owned one of the stores. It would be common knowledge soon enough. She waited for Will to say what they'd come to say. He managed to get it all out. The sheriff's eyebrows shot up and his mouth dropped open.

"Wal, I'll be a snake's elbow. That's what happens when I get stove up. All kinds of things go to hell." The shaggy eyebrows came down in a scowl. "I'd druther let the U.S. government enforce its own laws, but I'll sure do some lookin' around and ask some questions. Soon's I get this junk off of my leg."

"Think he'll do it?" Will asked as they walked back to the Dodge House.

"I'll see to it."

Grinning, Will said, "You're one lady I wouldn't want no trouble with."

She squeezed his arm. "Care to look at some catalogs with me, or would you rather go to the saloons and help

216

your cowboys celebrate?"

"Well, I oughta have at least one drink with 'em. Besides"—he grinned again—"I wanta see old China Eye—you remember China Eye—and see what he looks like when he gets slicked up."

Chuckling, Lucina said, "That should be interesting. I'd like to see him too."

He wasn't hard to see.

In front of the Dodge House, Will stopped so suddenly, Lucina took two steps beyond him before she realized he had stopped. "Good gawd a-mighty. It can't be. It is."

Coming toward them was the cowboy cook, grinning from ear to ear. He wore a new white hat that was almost as big as a Mexican sombrero, new boots with pull straps that hung down to the heels, California wool pants with the legs tucked inside the boots, a new blue satin shirt with pearl buttons, and a new polka-dot bandana around his neck. A barber had clipped the hair off the back of his neck and left it lady white. The hat covered his head down to his ears, and he could have been bald for all anyone could tell.

The only thing not new was the .44 Colt in a worn holster high on his right hip.

"Howdy folks," he said. Even his blank eye looked brighter.

"Gaw-ud damn. You look like a Christmas tree, China Eye. Lu, did you ever see anything like this?"

"You look very nice, Mr., uh, China Eye."

Still grinning, the cowboy cook said, "The lady knows a gentleman when she sees one. I don't know what she sees in a ragged counterfeit duck like you. If there was a church sociable around here I'd invite her to accompany me there."

"I'd go, too," Lucina said. "I'd be proud to accompany you."

"What're you gonna do next, China Eye? You can't go back to the wagon. Nobody'd see you there."

"Yes, you have to be seen to be appreciated, Mr. China Eye."

"Wal, since there ain't no church sociable, I reckon I'll pay my respects to the boys at the bar. Only for a few minutes, howsomever. If I can find one that's got a fiddler, I might stay long enough to listen to the music. I ain't hoed it down for a year or more, and I don't wanta forget how."

Lucina said, "Will, why don't you have a drink with him. You can find me at the hotel later."

"All right." To China Eye, he said, "I know I look like a rangy coyote beside you, but if you can stand it I'll buy you the first drink of whiskey you've had since we left home."

They turned to go. They didn't get far.

"Whups," said China Eye as he collided with another pedestrian on the plank walk.

"Whups, hell," said Marshal Jesse Vann. "What makes you Texans think you can hog the sidewalk. Get the hell out of my way."

"Just a minute here, Marshal," Will said.

"Yeah? You wanta get locked up again?"

China Eye said, "Let me handle 'im, Will. I'm the one he knocked into."

"Why you one-eyed old turkey, if you don't get off the sidewalk I'm gonna lock you up for drunk and disorderly."

"He hasn't had a drink in at least four months," Will said. "And you bumped into him."

"You callin' me a liar?" The marshal's hand was close to his gun butt again.

Lucina interrupted: "I'm a witness to anything that happens here. Keep that in mind, Marshal."

"You're gonna interfere with the law one time too many, lady. Now I want you cowboys off the street. In fact, I want you out of town. If I see you on the street again today I'm gonna lock up the whole kaboodle of you."

218

"You can try," China Eye said. "You ain't man enough to do it."

"What's that? Them's fightin' words. I don't have to take that."

With a one-eyed glance at Will, China Eye spoke through clenched teeth, "I smell somethin' that stinks, don't you, Will. This knothead is lookin' for a fight."

Lucina warned, "Don't antagonize him, China Eye. That's what he wants."

But China Eye continued, "Now me and Will here are goin' in that there saloon and havin' a drink of whiskey. Kindly step out of our way."

Mashal Jesse Vann stood straddle legged in the middle of the plank walk between the two men and the Longbranch Saloon. The cowboy cook tried to walk around him, but he couldn't do it without brushing shoulders. He was shoved roughly off the walk into the street. His hand went to the .44 in the worn holster.

The marshal's six-gun was instantly in his right hand, and before China Eye's gun cleared leather it popped.

China Eye sat down hard on the seat of his pants. A red splotch appeared in the center of the new blue satin shirt. Slowly, he toppled over on his side.

Will yelled, screamed, "You sonofabitch. You goddam sonofabitch." He grabbed for the pearl-handled Russian .44. Stopped. He was looking into the bore of the marshal's gun.

A cruel smile divided Jesse Vann's lips, "Go ahead, cowboy. Pull your fancy pistol. Go ahead."

The gunshot emptied the Longbranch. Cowboys ran out into the street to see what had happened. They stopped short when they saw their cook lying in the street and the marshal with a gun in his hand.

"What the holy hell's goin' on? Will, what happened?"

Will squatted before China Eye and turned him over onto his back. Clint Overhart squatted beside him. "He's dead, ain't he Will?"

Glumly, Will answered, "Yeah." Slowly, Clint stood and faced the marshal.

Jesse Vann looked at the men around him. A few townsmen had come running up, too. "He went for his gun. I had to shoot 'im." The marshal nodded at the dead cowboy's six-gun on the ground. "These damned Texans are always startin' fights."

"You're a liar." Clint Overhart stood in front of the marshal, his face set in hard lines and his hand on his gun butt. "Old China Eye never started a fight in his life. You're a goddamned liar."

"That's it." The marshal's face was red, and his eyes were wild. He glanced again at the men around him. "I don't have to take insults. Shuck your gun, cowboy." He still had the hogleg pistol in his hand, and he pointed it at Clint's chest.

"Make me."

"What?"

"I said make me, you low-life yellow-livered piece of cow manure."

"If you don't drop that gun belt I'll shoot you in the name of the law."

Clint put his hands on his hips and locked eyes with the marshal. "You ain't got guts enough to shoot a man that's lookin' at you."

"That did it." But the marshal couldn't meet Clint's hard gaze, and his eyes went to the cowboy's holstered gun. It was a fatal mistake.

No one knew Clint Overhart could move so fast. No one knew exactly what happened until later when they had time to think about it. But the cowboy's left hand shot out and grabbed the marshal's gun, pushed it aside just as it fired. In the same instant, a six-gun jumped into the cowboy's right hand. It too fired.

A look of surprised horror came over the lawman's face. His eyes rolled up into his head. His knees buckled. He fell face down. Clint stepped back and let him fall.

No one spoke for a long moment. No one moved. Then Will said calmly, "Clint, let's ride."

He borrowed a mount from one of the cowboys, and promised to be back soon. He rode out of town with Clint. At the Double O wagon, he told his uncle what had happened.

Lucas Porter swallowed a lump in his throat and said, "China Eye's dead?"

"Yeah."

It took the older Porter a full minute to absorb that. He stood with his head down. Then, "Clint, take any two horses you want out of the remuda. Here." He pulled a roll of bills out of a pants pocket and peeled off two fifties. "I'd head west if I was you. Get on the other side of them mountains. It don't make no difference who was right and who was wrong. You killed a lawman. That's all the law will think about."

"I'm obliged, Lucas." Clint caught two horses, put his bed and a few groceries on one and his saddle on the other. Mounted, he paused. "I'm not sorry for what I did. I'm only sorry for China Eye. He was a good man." Clint Overhart rode away at a fast trot, heading west.

Chapter Twenty-Seven

The morning after China Eye was killed they wrapped his body in new blankets and buried him in his new clothes in a new cemetery. A town handman was paid to carve his name, his real name—James Buckholder—on a wooden headboard. The Double O cowboys gathered around the grave while Lucas Porter tried to recite the Twenty-third Psalm. They stood with their hats off, heads bowed, hair blowing in the prairie wind. Will tried to remember the Lord's Prayer his mother had taught him long ago. He stuttered and stammered, but recited most of it. When his voice choked, Lucina put an arm around his waist and put her face against his shoulder.

Then the Double O pulled out, crossing the river at noon. The wagon was driven by a cowboy who had been appointed cook. The remuda followed the wagon. Loose horses splashed playfully across the river, seeming to be happy about going back to Texas. Will stayed behind, promising to catch up. "Don't look for me until you see me coming," he told his uncle.

In her room, Lucina stood in front of Will, her face solemn. "We're going our separate ways, aren't we, Will."

He tried to grin. "I'd make a sorry store clerk."

"And I'd be a terrible ranch wife." She was pensive a

222

moment, then, "Will we ever see each other again?"

"You bet. I'm gonna take my share of your granddad's loot and my wages and the money my folks left and put together another herd. I'll be back here next spring."

"You're going into business for yourself, then?"

"Yup. I might lose my britches, but I'm gonna give 'er a try."

"Meanwhile, you promised to look at some catalogs with me."

They had a noon meal and looked at catalogs. They had supper and looked at catalogs. Will gave her the best advice he could: "I wouldn't stock too many saddles. Cowboys like to have their saddles made to order. But things that wear out, like cinches—mohair is the best—and latigos, and boots—be sure they have a strong shank for comfort in a stirrup—and blankets. Those Levi britches are everybody's favorite nowadays, but a cowboy likes to dress up in good wool pants too. Guns, whatever is the latest invention from Colt and Smith & Wesson and Winchester, but .44s or .45s. Cowboys think self-cocking revolvers are sissy, and . . ."

Until finally long after dark she put the catalogs aside and pulled him to his feet. "You can kiss me if you want to." He did, shyly at first, then when she pressed against him, long and hard. It was the most exciting thing he'd ever done in his life and he didn't want to quit.

But he had to breathe. She had to breathe. She said, "You don't need to catch up to your crew tonight, do you?"

"Naw."

"Well." She was hesitant. "I've never before met a man I wanted to, uh . . ."

And then, "Oh, shucksdammit, we're adults, aren't we?"

It was dusk a day later when he caught up with the Double O wagon. As he rode he recalled everything

223

that had happened since the outfit had left the home ranch. It was sad what had happened to China Eye. But he'd do it again. Putting together a big herd of cattle, driving them to Dodge City, would be a financial risk. It would be dangerous.

But he had to go back to Dodge. Remembering last night, he grinned.

Nothing could keep him away.